The Forgotten People

By
Barbara Custer

Night to Dawn Magazine & Books LLC
P. O. Box 643
Abington, PA 19001
www.bloodredshadow.com

Print ISBN: 978-1-937769-53-6
Digital ISBN: 978-1-937769-54-3

Cover Illustrator: L. M. Labat
Editor: Esther Mitchell

Printed in the United States of America
Worldwide Electronic & Digital Rights
1st North American, Australian and UK
Print Rights

To Michael, who left this world much too soon. Love you forever.

I would like to thank Esther Mitchell for all the work and patience she demonstrated during the editing process to prepare The Forgotten People for publication. Hugs go out to my fellow scribes at the Hatboro Writers Group for their good humor and support with my writing, and to the Writer's Coffeehouse for their advice on publishing and marketing.

Finally, to L. M. Labat, thank you for designing a lovely wraparound cover.

Table of Contents

Introduction

Henry David Thoreau once wrote "If a man does not keep pace with his companions, perhaps it is because he hears a different drummer."

Perhaps such music might come from a place where the boundaries are so thin, anything can happen.

As I wrote these tales, it crossed my mind how all of the protagonists had something in common. None of them fit in with their peers. Events beyond their control made them pariahs. I asked myself: what if their circumstances changed? One character might discover a wormhole to an alternate world, while another rescues an injured alien. How would such changes affect others' behavior toward them?

Of people who march to a different drummer, Thoreau says, "Let him step to the music which he hears, however measured or far away."

And so, gentle reader, I'd like to introduce you to the music each character hears.

Shall we dance?

Popple Land

"Stop it, --you're hurting me!" As the needle penetrated his wrist, Eric Gilmore's face contorted into a grimace, freckles standing out on his pale cheeks.

Respiratory Therapist Chloe Scythe knelt by the bed, probing for his elusive artery. The doctors ordered an arterial blood draw to diagnose his breathing difficulty. Hands gripping his wrist, fingers on his throbbing pulse, she advanced and withdrew the needle. Why couldn't she get the blood?

"Ow!" Gilmore's scream impinged on her concentration. "What are you doing?"

Chloe's surroundings blurred, and a softer, familiar face replaced the angry one before her. He had the same almond eyes and wavy hair, but his arms sought her like a drowning man reaching for a life preserver.

Tears burned Chloe's eyes and ran down her cheeks. Dropping the needle, she cradled his hands in hers.

"Mark!" she sobbed, unaware of the bruise budding on his wrist. "I'm sorry I hurt you."

"Get out!" Gilmore wrenched his arm free. "Get someone who knows what they're doing."

Why is he yelling at me? Chloe brushed wisps of oily blonde hair from her damp forehead. "What's wrong? I said I was......"

The door behind her opened.

"What's going on in here?" A woman wearing a plaid suit marched into the room, arms hugging her chart. Her name tag said *Marian Williams, M.D.*

"This nut tried to butcher me." Gilmore jerked his thumb toward Chloe. "She thinks I'm some guy named Mark."

"I see." Doctor Williams' ruby lips pursed in a tight frown. "Chloe, why are you calling him Mark? Didn't you check his I.D. bracelet?"

"Yes." Chloe stared at Gilmore. How *could* she confuse his stony face and scowl with the man she loved? "You ordered an arterial blood test on Mr. Gilmore."

"That's right." Doctor Williams nodded. "Eric, you've developed pneumonia. You've had problems breathing, so I ordered a blood test to evaluate your oxygen levels."

"You're right about the breathing." Gilmore coughed and spat something into a tissue. He leaned forward in bed, shoulders hunched. "Get someone else to do the test."

Doctor Williams inspected his wrist. A bump the size of a half-dollar had erupted, surrounded by purple rose petals. Chloe hugged herself, shivering. According to Doctor Williams, his low platelet count prohibited effective clotting, leaving Gilmore prone to bruises.

Doctor Williams gave Chloe a censuring stare. "Page Denise Mueller."

"I can't." Chloe lowered her eyes, not caring to involve her supervisor. "She's in a meeting."

"Never mind," Doctor Williams snapped in annoyance. "I'll call her myself. You may go."

Chloe shuffled to the door, eyes focused on Gilmore. "Can I get you anything?"

"I said you may go," Doctor Williams ordered. "You've done enough."

Chloe shrank in fear. Things like this never happened before her husband Mark died last year. Doctor Williams and her staff used to smile and strike up a conversation with her. Six months ago, they might have nodded "hello." Now, their pointed fingers and hushed whispers followed her like a bunch of tin cans tied to a dog's tail, finding fault with everything she did. Now, the doctor's gaze drilled into the back of her neck, full of criticism and speculation.

Too much. The sounds of Doctor Williams' harsh voice and Gilmore's yell were too much to take. Chloe's breath hitched with sobs as she scurried to a restroom.

Standing before a mirror, she scrubbed her tear-streaked face. Dark circles shadowed her eyes. She couldn't recall when she last got a decent night's sleep. Her pink scrubs and lab coat swam around her bony frame. She lost thirty pounds since Mark's death.

****

Chloe's cell phone rang just as her shift ended, and the screen displayed Management's office number. She rubbed her arms, trying to soothe the frightened gooseflesh running along her skin as she shuffled to the respiratory department.

In the back office, Denise Mueller sat at her desk, leafing through a file. Framed pictures of Denise's family invited friendly conversation, but her knotted brows and frown warned Chloe she was in serious trouble.

"Have a seat." Denise rose and moved around her desk to push the door shut behind Chloe. "Russell will join us shortly."

With a deep sigh, Chloe flopped into a leather chair. "Is this about Eric Gilmore?"

"Yes. Doctor Williams sent me a memo." Denise's somber tone and tear-filled eyes tightened the fist of fear in Chloe's gut. *Why the hell is she crying? She's not the one in trouble.* Chloe propped her arms on the desk, elbowing the pictures aside. "Williams always complains about me."

"She had a good reason. One day, you'll work yourself out of a job." Denise heaved a sigh. "Why did you call Mr. Gilmore Mark?"

"I don't know." Chloe's shoulders slumped. Her gaze shifted toward the door. "It just happened. I'm sorry."

"Apology accepted. I get you're still grieving over Mark. It doesn't excuse your technique for drawing blood." Denise's eyes flashed with anger. "Anyone can miss, but continued probing can damage the artery and surrounding nerves."

A horrible wave of shame washed through Chloe, leaving a burning sensation in the back of Chloe's throat. She licked her lips.

"You didn't hold the vessel," Denise continued. "That's unacceptable, especially with someone like Gilmore. Because of his low platelet count, it takes longer for his blood to clot."

Chloe froze as Denise's statement jarred her back to Mount Carmel Hospital, two years ago. Her meeting with Doctor Daniels about Mark.

"Doctor, Mark's not doing well. He's getting pale, and his gums are bleeding."

Doctor Daniels threw a cursory glance at Mark, then shrugged. "I warned you that the chemotherapy would cause side effects."

"Don't worry, hon, I'll make it." Mark smiled, and blood oozed from the side of his lips. He patted Chloe's shoulder with his bruised hand.

"Look at the bleeding!"

"You should expect that," Daniels' perfunctory tone grated on Chloe's overwrought nerves. "Because of his low platelet count, it takes longer for his blood to clot."

"Are you listening?" Denise's stern voice invaded Chloe's thoughts. "Gilmore will die without a bone marrow transplant."

"Bone marrow transplant?" Chloe echoed feebly. *Mark needed a transplant, too, but he couldn't find a suitable donor.*

"Eric's got no siblings. His father died five years

ago, and his mother's leukocyte antigens don't match. He's all his mother has, and she's taking this hard. The chances of finding someone through the registry are almost nil. Even with the transplant, he could have..."

A knock at the door drew both their attentions as Russell Long, the department director, stepped inside. Salt and pepper hair surrounded his angular face. With his thick mustache and gray business suit, he reminded Chloe of Adolf Hitler.

Russell cleared his throat. "Sorry to keep you waiting."

Denise looked up at Russell. "I spoke to Chloe about Eric."

"Good." Contempt dripped in Russell's tone. "Did you mention the missed treatments and sloppy assessments?"

Russell ticked off Chloe's offenses on his fingers, "Incorrect doses and missed treatments. Inappropriate settings on ventilators and other oxygen devices. Meantime, you walk the floors in a trance, calling anyone who even remotely resembles your late husband Mark."

Chloe dragged clammy fingers through her hair. "Wait a minute. You never told me any of this."

"Denise and I sent you memos. Obviously, you haven't checked your mail bin." Reaching into his jacket, Russell pulled out a stack of memos. He dumped them on the desk in front of Chloe. "Take a look."

Tears welled up in Chloe's eye, blurring her vision, as she clenched and unclenched her fists. "You think I'm so rotten? Fire me."

"I should have fired you long ago, but I cut you a break because of your recent loss. My patience is wearing thin."

Chloe's gaze dropped to the framed pictures. Jumping up, she gripped the desk, knuckles turning white.

"You've both got surviving spouses and parents," she shouted, voice choking with sobs. "I don't. My parents died when I was in college, and you know about Mark. So back off."

Denise's lower lip puckered and her eyes moistened with tears. "I've had my problems, too," she said. "I've had to take intermittent family leave because my mom's got severe emphysema. She may die soon."

Chloe drew in a sharp breath. "I'm sorry to hear that. How do you manage to concentrate?"

"I try to approach the patient the way I hope people will treat my mom." Denise's voice softened. "Know what makes disciplining you so hard? You used to go out of your way to help people. At one time, I considered hiring you to look after my mom. But this past year, it's like you wandered into some black hole where no one can reach you."

Denise paused to scribble notes in Chloe's file. "I thought a patient like Mark would restore your caring instincts."

"So much for your amateur psychology." Russell heaved a heavy sigh. "What should we do, Chloe?"

"I don't know." Chloe gulped, her throat bone dry.

Denise laid her pudgy hand on Chloe's arm. "Go easy on her, Russell. She's hurting."

"In other words, look the other way until her errors cost someone's life." Russell's eyes narrowed. "Chloe, a time comes when you must bury the dead and get on with your life."

Yeah, yeah, yeah. Try doing it sometime. Sticking her forefinger into her mouth, Chloe bit her nail to the quick.

"Human Resources offers employee counseling. I insist you get help." Russell handed Chloe a business card. "Rose Carter's number. She runs the program."

"Okay."

"No more rotations through the critical care floors. Stay away from Eric Gilmore." He cut his gaze toward Denise. "I trust you'll make up the assignments accordingly."

Denise nodded, making more notes in the folder. "I'll write this up as a verbal warning, too."

"Make that a written warning." Russell nodded in self-confirmation. "You may go, Chloe. Denise and I need to talk privately."

Chloe backed toward the door. After wiping her tear-streaked face, she muddled through her shift report, clocked out, and fled to her battered Ford, parked in the hospital garage.

With a tearful sigh, she inspected her car's crumbled fenders—grim reminders of how grief distracted her on the road. Last time she exited the expressway, she almost totaled her car. Since then, she took the back roads — narrow streets snaking through woods -- to work.

****

As she drove, the dull ache settling between her temples reminded Chloe she missed lunch. She was unable to even think about food after her run-in with Doctor Williams. *I don't think I had breakfast, either. I'll stop at a deli on the way home.*

Sometime later, she exited the woods and happened upon *Sam's Hoagies*. Cars and pedestrians crowded the parking lot because of an outside art sale, so Chloe parked on a side street and walked the block back to the store. On the way, she bypassed clusters of statues and framed paintings on folding tables. Nostalgia tugged at her. She used to love browsing through art galleries. Now, she kept her eyes on the deli. With her job in jeopardy, she dared not let herself be tempted.

Nearly to the deli, she stumbled to an abrupt stop, gasping, as a painting grabbed her attention in spite of her efforts to ignore the artwork around her.

Years ago, the attraction would not have surprised Chloe. Before Mark got sick, she used to sketch still life and take art classes. Her interest in drawing and her desire to help the sick died along with Mark. None of which mattered now. The painting called to Chloe, driving away all memory of her disciplinary meeting. She forgot about her job misery, about missed meals, and about loss. She forgot everything except the painting — a street scene titled *Popple Land* — resplendent in pinks, reds, and gold hues.

"Oh, my God, it's beautiful!"

A three-feet-square portrait, *Popple Land* portrayed a woman walking down a slate-paneled street. Her features and blonde hair gave her a human shape, but her canary yellow eyes and albino complexion named her extraterrestrial. Dozens of heart-shaped balloons — at least they looked like the Mylar balloons Chloe saw at stores — danced on tethers from poles along the path. A bell-shaped aircraft studded with rainbow lights stood at the end of the road, but Chloe's eyes settled on the woman's red-beaded tunic.

The price tag on the painting's wooden frame read $100.

"I can't afford this," Chloe murmured to herself. "I could lose my job tomorrow."

Her body wasn't listening to her brain. Her bony arms reached for the painting, despite her self-admonishment. The bulky picture felt light in her arms. In a daze, Chloe walked toward the artist and his assistant at the booth. She removed a credit card from her wallet with trembling digits and handed it over to complete the sale. After walking her purchase back to the car, she returned to buy a ham sandwich at *Sam's*.

****

Chloe's Ford rumbled up her street and puttered to a stop in front of her house. Hugging her purchases to herself, Chloe shuffled up the sidewalk to her three-bedroom ranch house. Mark bought the house. They talked about filling the house with children until leukemia shit-canned their plans.

Shoving open the front door, she set down the painting and rubbed her arms, trying to soothe sudden chills. The cheer inspired by *Popple Land* was chased by the gloom of coming home to an empty house. A year's distance between Mark's death and now still didn't make it any easier.

In the living room, the shivers drew a hard line of ice up to Chloe's neck, lifting the hairs there. She ran her fingers along her Ethan Allen furniture and dust-covered tables as she imagined her mother-in-law, Klara, barging in, face wrinkled in a censuring scowl.

"Look at this filthy house. No wonder Mark got sick!"

"Doctor Daniels said ..."

"The heck with Doctor Daniels. You should have gotten a second opinion. But you didn't because you married Mark for his money. You couldn't wait to bleed him dry."

Chloe's breath sawed audibly in and out as the memory played through her mind. Spinning on her heel, she slammed the door shut and locked it tight against the return of past intrusions.

"Mark's mother can't hurt you now," she scolded herself.

Still, it was impossible to forget the hate in Klara's eyes. Giving Klara updates on Mark's condition was cold work. The chill spread from the woman in all directions, and even Chloe's warmest coat couldn't take away the bitter chill of it.

Rubbing her arms again, Chloe moved the *Popple Land* painting against the wall facing her marble fireplace. Turning toward the brass-framed painting hanging above the mantle, she faced a portrait of her and Mark posed by the church doors and clad in their wedding clothes. Lifting the wedding portrait from the wall, she cradled it in her arms as she headed for the kitchen.

A full moon rose in the darkening sky outside, casting eerie shadows on her porcelain-tiled floor. The marble-top table and countertops looked as barren as her life. After Mark died, she tried to move on—really, she did. She even took another art class, hoping to meet new people. Only, shades and forms no longer interested her. Still, she would have sat through anything to make friends. It never happened. After class, everyone rushed home to their own lives, leaving Chloe feeling more alone than ever.

Swallowing two aspirins, Chloe brewed coffee and unwrapped her sandwich. Between nibbles, she pulled a manila envelope containing her prior years' work evaluations from a drawer under the counter. Each file included citations for her clinical assessments, some of which saved lives. She read these memos every night, hoping to recapture the spark of motivation. It never worked. Her downhill performance and complaints from the staff continued, and she couldn't seem to make herself care.

"Your days as a respiratory therapist are finished," she admitted to herself. "Good thing you've got savings and Mark's life insurance. God help you when that runs out."

With an empty shrug, Chloe stuffed the evaluations back into the envelope. As she did, a yellow sheet slid out of the pile. Its heading read "Mount Carmel Hospital."

A gasp flew from Chloe as she snatched it up and lifted it to the light.

The document listed her blood type, antigen class, and other information marking her as a potential marrow donor. She initially took the test as a last-ditch effort to save Mark.

"I'd forgotten about my being A-negative." Eric Gilmore received numerous Type A-negative blood transfusions. Could her marrow help him?

"Get real. The chances of compatibility are... Forget it." She tossed the paper into the trash.

As she looked down at Mark's portrait, heartbroken sobs strangled Chloe. Mark would understand her pain. His love gave her the confidence to work in intensive care settings, and to speak out when something was wrong. Her inspiration for both died with him.

"Oh, Mark," she wept, hugging the portrait to her chest. "Why did you leave me?"

A thrumming noise filtered in from her living room. It sounded like faraway jet engines. The thrumming grew louder and a floral scent filled her nostrils. Her heart hammered in her chest.

Oh, my God, did I leave the door open for burglars?

She set the portrait on her kitchen table with trembling hands and, swallowing hard, forced herself back into the living room. At the doorway, something soft as a kitten's paw brushed her face.

It was a heart-shaped balloon, covered with white lace. The shiny plastic looked like Mylar.

Chloe darted a glance toward her windows — both closed and locked. Since Mark's passing, she never bothered opening the windows. Her trailing glance crossed the balloon again, then moved down the ivory wall toward the painting. A startled gasp flew from her. Something changed. The blonde stood where she was, gazing at the spacecraft, but now it appeared someone sketched in a young man holding a sandwich.

Her breaths panting in fear, Chloe knelt before the painting, watching the images dissolve into layered shades of old paint. Above the faces stretched the bluish hues of sky, done in quick layered down strokes of the artist's brush. White and red heart balloon shapes were sketched in between these strokes.

Chloe reached for the balloon, which drifted by the window, and held it up to the painting. The colors matched.

"What the hell? No one ever buys me balloons or perfume." She scratched the back of her head, then shrugged. No doubt the combination of car accidents, Russell's criticisms, and months of grief provided fertile grounds for hallucinations.

Rising to her feet, she turned toward the kitchen. "I'd better get some sleep."

As she returned to the kitchen, screams blasted from her living room.

Chloe jumped, her body trembling like a wire. She froze, unsure what she should do. Another scream followed, and her instinct to help took over. She dashed back into the living room. Her sofa, two chairs, and fireplace appeared intact. The screaming persisted, but the thrumming stopped. A stiff wind slapped her cheeks, blowing hair into her eyes.

As she turned toward the window, Chloe's breath stuck in her throat. Either her window was gone, or the wall had become one large window. In any case, she no longer saw her Ford parked outside. Instead, the blonde woman from the painting stood near her street, crying for help. Beside her, the young man splayed his hands around his neck in a universal choking gesture. His blond hair wavered like plankton in the wind. Some of the balloons broke loose from their posts and drifted into Chloe's living room, where pieces of uneaten bread lay scattered on her rug.

Another cry for help split the air. The wind howled, but Chloe focused on the young man who was turning blue. The hem of her lab coat fluttered against her pant legs as she walked toward the picture now covering the wall, floor to ceiling and side to side. The wind blew at her clothes, and she smelled cologne again.

"Oh, my God!" she cried, rushing up to the painting.

"No more rotations through the critical care floors," Russell's voice echoed in her mind.

Russell can go to hell, she decided. Just five feet away, the young man lurched in the street, gasping for air. His companion gazed at him with wide, frightened eyes.

Taking a deep breath, Chloe raced into the picture.

The air was chilly, and the bobbing balloons rubbed her cheeks. She barely noticed them as she stepped up behind the man and laced her arms around his waist. She thrust inward, jamming her thumb knuckles up against his gut just below the ribs. Morsels of food flew from his mouth. The man slumped to the ground, gasping and dripping with sweat.

She glanced over her shoulder, expecting to see her living room. It was gone. Lace-coated red balloons tethered to metal poles made shushing noises in the breeze. Behind the poles, she saw a laptop computer propped on a stool.

The screen facing Chloe was the same size as the painting she bought near *Sam's Hoagies* and showed her living room as seen from the wall she just went through. Her gaze skated toward the woman beside her. The woman's posture and height were similar to her own. Goosebumps erupted on her arms.

I saved a man's life. First time since...

A cold hand brushed her calf, yanking a small scream from her throat.

"I'm sorry, I didn't mean to frighten you." The young man's weak voice was laced with genuine regret. "Whatever you did ... worked. I feel much better."

"It's called the Heimlich maneuver," Chloe told him. "I learned it in school."

The woman stepped forward. For the first time, Chloe noticed a silver pin with symbols on her tunic. "I owe you, Chloe, for saving my brother."

"I'm glad I could help. How did you know... how did I get here?"

The woman raised her tunic, showing three white scars on her right knee. "You found a door to a parallel world. I, too, lost my husband to an incurable disease. Afterward, I became accident-prone. I fell from a lift and tore my knee."

Chloe hiked her pant leg. It was the left instead of the right knee, but the scars, left by a car crash, were the same. A horrible observation filtered through her mind. Her companion wore the emblem over her right bosom. Chloe wore her name tag over her left.

Except for eye color and complexion, the woman facing the spacecraft was her mirror image.

"You're me, aren't you? What should I call you?"

"Your society's fixation with names amuses me." Her companion smiled. "Althea, if it will make you feel better. I know about you because people like me can read auras. Your grief led you here. This meeting is destiny."

"Destiny?" Chloe shivered at the hissing wind. Tiny blonde curls waved from Althea's forehead, glittering like filaments of gold. She shifted her gaze toward the young man, who was still breathing hard. "You should take your brother to a doctor. He may have aspirated something. I'll go with you if you'd like."

"Thank you, but I'll manage. You must return to your world. Someone there needs your help."

"Who?" Chloe arched her brows.

"I think you already know." Althea retrieved a crumpled paper from her side pocket. "You threw this out by mistake. I got it while you were helping my brother."

"Thank you." Chloe accepted the paper. She turned toward the row of balloon trees. The computer was gone, and the screen had grown to enormous size. It still showed her living room.

"Go on." Althea touched the back of her head.

Chloe took several steps toward the screen and could hear traffic. The balloons brushed her shoulders, making soft, smacking sounds.

Maybe one day, I'll move here. If I lose my job.

"Please hurry," Althea pleaded. "Your timing will determine his chances for survival."

Eyes shut, Chloe lunged forward, convinced she'd run into shattering glass. Instead, she tripped and sprawled onto her living room floor, still clutching the paper.

Chloe scrambled to her feet and spread the paper in her hand out against the wall before her.

"My blood test. I think Althea wants me to give this to Mr. Gilmore's doctor."

She paced around the room, staring at the page in her hands. What should she do with the test results? Pausing at the window, she stared at the moonlit sky. Images of Gilmore's pale face swam through her mind.

What will you do? His mocking voice whispered from the recesses of her mind. *Let me die? Like Mark?*

"No way," she said aloud. "I can't let this go."

****

The next day

After her morning rounds, Chloe headed to the Intensive Care Unit. No one sat at the nurses' station, but Doctor Williams was with a patient. Chloe scrunched behind the door of the utility room and waited. Peeping through the crack, she watched Williams exit the patient's room and sit at the desk. While Williams charted and wrote orders, Chloe tiptoed to the counter.

Nervous—aware her offer could be instantly rejected—she pulled the slip from her pocket and held it out. "Doctor, would you look at these test results?"

Doctor Williams reached for her blue-rimmed glasses. "Which test?"

Chloe laid her report on the desk blotter. "I heard Eric Gilmore needs a bone marrow transplant. Does this test show compatibility?"

"It might if the HLA..." Williams' head jerked up, and she arched her eyebrows. "Wait a minute. What's going on here?"

Chloe hugged herself, shivering. Coming here disobeyed Russell's orders and Williams knew it. Pulse pounding in her throat, she regretted purchasing *Popple Land*. The cost of the painting could pay her electric bill.

Popple Land offers happiness. The defiant thought flew through her mind. *I could live there.*

Spurred forward by the thought, she stepped closer to Williams' side. *You can do this, Chloe. Eric Gilmore's survival depends on you.*

"I want to know if my bone marrow could help Mr. Gilmore." Hands propped against the desk hard enough for her knuckles to turn white, she clenched her jaw to stop her teeth from chattering.

Doctor Williams' bespectacled eyes narrowed. "I haven't got time for this nonsense. I'm calling Russell Long right now."

Chloe lifted her fists against her trembling lips. The goose bumps forming on her neck didn't surprise her, but the thought going through her head did.

Althea wouldn't let this tin goddess intimidate her. Why am I?

Smoldering anger reared its head, driving away Chloe's shivering. "Have you ever lost anyone to cancer?"

"Not that it's your business, but no." Doctor Williams glanced at the phone and sighed.

"Good for you." Chloe's voice started as a whisper and built into a shrill, furious crescendo. "My husband died of acute myelogenous leukemia last summer. A transplant might have saved him, but we couldn't find a matching donor. I noticed Eric Gilmore has the same blood type as mine, so I thought I'd let you know I'm willing to donate. If you want to report me for that, go ahead."

Turning on her heels, Chloe strode down the hall, reaching into her left pocket for the envelope containing her resignation as she did.

She'd rather quit than be fired.

She suspected it would take more than Williams' temper to make Althea quit, and then another thought went through her head.

You think Popple Land is a sanctuary from your problems. Is that wise?

Anything was better than slaving here.

"Chloe, wait!"

Chloe bolted to the steel gray elevators at the sound of Williams' angry voice, behind her. She zigzagged around the stretchers cluttering the hall, willing to do anything to escape the clicking rush of high-heeled feet heralding confrontation in pursuit.

"Chloe!" She nearly paused as she realized Williams' voice bled with desperation, not anger. "Where did you take this test?"

"Mount Carmel Hospital." Chloe ducked around a cement pillar, saw patients and their escorts cluttering the elevators, and sprinted to a door marked *Exit*. "Forget I said anything."

"I can't. Your histocompatibility antigens—at least the major ones—match Gilmore's."

Chloe collapsed against the door, gasping for breath. For the moment, thoughts of Althea eased her panic.

No, it's not Althea. You're doing this, yourself. No matter how the rest of this conversation turns out, remember Eric Gilmore's life is at stake.

"They do?" She faced the doctor directly.

"I'd like to do a repeat study." Doctor Williams' somber gaze assessed her. "Do you know what a bone marrow transplant involves?"

Chloe nodded. "You'll have to stick needles in my back to harvest the marrow. Don't worry. I can handle it."

"There are other ways to do a transplant, but even so, Gilmore has only a thirty percent chance for a cure." Williams didn't mince words. "He could have serious complications, like infection or graft-versus-host disease."

Chloe dropped her gaze to the floor, hoping Williams wouldn't see her tears.

"I'm not trying to discourage you," Doctor Williams continued. "Gilmore's young. He has a real chance of beating this. His pneumonia is clearing, and he'll finish his first round of chemotherapy soon. Now's the time to consider a transplant."

Chloe nodded. Her past research on leukemia taught her Gilmore's best chance of success was after his first remission. "If I go through with this, please don't tell him."

"The donor's name remains confidential." Williams smiled, her voice softening. "How soon can you take the blood test?"

Time slipped away from Chloe. She felt adrift, uncertain.

Think about Popple Land. Think about Althea and how she looked. She's not afraid of anything; even with her husband dead and brother hurt, she could... "take on anything," she murmured aloud.

"Pardon?" Williams leaned forward.

"I said, I can take it after I finish my shift."

Williams straightened with a sigh. "Now would be better. Would you mind if I spoke with Denise about arranging coverage for you?"

Chloe shrugged. "No."

She stood hugging her papers while Williams made the call, then followed the doctor to the laboratory adjacent to the intensive care unit. When the technician called her to the desk, Chloe rolled up her sleeve and held out her right arm. Her mind drifted to Popple Land and its balloon trees while the blood filled the barrel. Blood drawn, she went back to her assigned floors, and promptly forgot about the test and its implications.

At 2:30 — an hour before quitting time — Denise summoned her to the office. Chills raced through Chloe. *What have I done now?*

Denise ushered her into her office, and the memory of her blood test rushed back at the sight of Doctor Williams, standing by the desk, smiling.

"You're a perfect match," the doctor informed her. "Are you still willing to donate?"

Chloe nodded. "You're going to have to stick a needle into my pelvic bone, right?"

"What I have in mind is a stem cell donation. This seems to work best for adults. A technician will run your blood through a machine to draw out the stem cells, and the solution will be infused into Eric. There will be no need for surgery."

"Okay. When do you want to do this infusion?"

"Before I do anything, you'll need to go to the lab daily for the next five days for injections of Neupogen to stimulate the growth of your white blood cells. You'll need a physical, too."

"No problem. I'll make an appointment with my family doctor."

"I'd rather you see a doctor on staff here. One of the ICU senior residents can examine you. If your exam and blood work yields no surprises, we should be able to do the infusion next Wednesday. I'll have my secretary call you with the times for the injections and other details." She drew in a deep breath. "I recommend you have someone drive you the day of the infusion."

Chloe contemplated the hushed whispers and pointed stares she endured at the hospital and shook her head. "I'll get a cab."

Williams arched her brows. "Don't you have a neighbor or a sibling?"

"She does," Denise interjected. "I'll make sure that Chloe gets to the hospital and home safely."

"Very well, then." Smiling, Williams left the office.

"Denise!" Chloe stared at her supervisor in shock. "I'm surprised you're willing to help, but I appreciate it. Thank you."

"Don't mention it." Admiration crept into Denise's voice. The censoring frown she had worn was gone, replaced by a genuine smile. "What you're doing takes guts. That's the Chloe I remember. I'll do anything to help you get back on track—role-playing, tutoring, whatever it takes."

****

The next five days passed in a blur. Chloe's back and thighs ached, a side effect of the Neupogen. The morning of the infusion, Denise showed up to drive her to the hospital. In the dressing room, Chloe put on a blue gown; then followed Denise and a nurse into the donation room. After she got into bed, Denise pulled up a chair beside her. Chloe lay quiet while the nurse placed an IV into the back of her left hand, then another into the crook of her right elbow. It was only a pinch, but the pain made Chloe think about the incident with Gilmore's blood test in ICU. She averted her gaze, shame pulsing through her.

"Are you okay?" Denise asked.

Chloe nodded. She held still while the nurse plugged the IV tubes into a centrifuge by the bed. Blood flowed from Chloe's right arm and into the machine. A whirling sound followed while the device spun the blood, separating her stem and white blood cells, which dripped as a creamy mixture into a plastic bag. The rest of her blood returned to her body through the tube in her left hand. The process would take about three hours.

Chloe waited until the nurse stepped out to answer. "I was thinking about what you could do to help me improve my work. The counselor suggested I keep a diary, so it might help if you could review my work daily so I could see what kind of mistakes I make, when I make them, and what was happening when I did it."

"Sure. We can do that when Doctor Williams okays your return to work."

"Why do I need her okay? I'm not sick."

"True, but your platelet count will be low after donating. Doctor Williams might not want you working right away."

"I see." Chloe shrugged. *At least it's paid leave. I still have to deal with the elephant in the room.*

She drew in another breath. "When the nurse stuck me, she got me to thinking about Gilmore's blood test. I'm so sorry that happened. If someone had done that to Mark, I would have been devastated."

"I'm sorry, too." Denise's voice softened.

****

Once the infusion was complete and the IVs removed, Chloe hopped out of bed, eager to dress and leave. Instead, a horrible wave of dizziness rolled through her, pitching her forward.

"Whoa!" Denise jumped to catch Chloe. "You'd better sit."

"Guess so." Chloe sat leaning forward, rubbing her head as a dull ache settled between her temples. "I'm not feeling so good. My head hurts. Doctor Williams warned me about headaches and dizziness, but yikes, the room's spinning."

"Some people get it more than others," the nurse informed her from the bio-hazard container where she dumped the IV tubing. "I'll be back with Tylenol and crackers."

"Tylenol?" Chloe looked up at Denise. "I've got aspirin in my purse."

"Doctor Williams won't want you taking aspirin until your cells regenerate. I'll get you Tylenol on the way home."

Why is she so being so kind? Never mind, I'll take it. I feel too crappy to drive to any pharmacy. Chloe resisted the urge to frown, managing a smile, instead. "I appreciate that."

Moments later, the nurse returned with Tylenol and discharge instructions. "You may have headaches or muscle pain, but you can take Motrin or Tylenol. You might notice you bruise more easily, but this should go away as your platelets return to normal. Get lots of rest. No strenuous activity for 48 hours."

"When may I go back to work?"

"You may go back to work in seven days."

Seven days? Chloe glanced at Denise.

"Go ahead and sign the discharge paper." Denise smiled, offering encouragement. "Just bring a copy when you come back to work."

"Okay." After signing the paperwork, Chloe rose carefully from the bed and dressed. She then shuffled to the car with Denise's arm for support.

Along the way home, Denise stopped at a store, returning to the car with a bag of groceries.

"Here you go." She handed the bag to Chloe. "Tylenol, Motrin, and a pint of chicken soup."

Tears blurred Chloe's gaze. She couldn't remember the last time someone was this kind to her. "Thank you."

At home, Chloe ate the soup, then headed to the sofa, but shook her head. "I'm not up to *Popple Land* today."

She went to bed, instead.

****

A gentle hand shook Chloe awake, to find a familiar blonde woman standing over her, brandishing a bouquet of pink-laced heart-shaped balloons. Despite the dimly lit room, Althea's blue sequins glittered. Shock plunged through Chloe.

What the heck is she doing in my bedroom?

Her visitor chuckled. "Why are you staring? Don't you recognize me?"

Chloe rubbed her eyes. Maybe she was dreaming.

"I never thanked you for rescuing my brother, so I hope these will do." Althea tied the bouquet to Chloe's bedpost.

Chloe inhaled deeply, savoring a floral scent. The lace poking from the balloon ties was satiny smooth. "How did you get here?"

"I crossed the border to your world the way you did to mine. Your house is tiny compared to our buildings, so finding my way around was easy." Althea smiled. "Your aura looks brighter now."

"My what?"

"I told you, I read people's auras. I heard you and your friend talking about Eric Gilmore. Something about a bone marrow transplant. Now that you completed your mission, we can move onto other things. For starters, the way you grieve over your husband."

At the mention of the word *husband,* Chloe's throat tightened and her vision blurred.

"Please, don't go there." Her voice came out a muffled sob. *Too late. Every time someone mentions Mark, I go to pieces.*

"I've lived there." Althea's voice softened. "I know people bombarded you with sermons about getting on with life. I've heard them, too."

Chloe nodded, shoulders shaking. "How did you get past it?"

"I was fortunate enough to have my brother. You don't have support, so after your husband died, your business went sour."

Chloe nodded, wiping tears from her eyes. "I don't have a business. I work for a hospital. After Mark died, I made some big mistakes and hurt my patients. It's like the part of me that cared about people died."

"You blame yourself for Mark's death."

"No, leukemia killed him. His mother holds me responsible, though. She said if I kept the house cleaner, Mark would have gotten better. She said it to me the day of the funeral and later when she came to the house to pick up some things Mark wanted her to have."

"Maybe her accusations made you think you don't deserve success." Althea smoothed back Chloe's hair with gentle, comforting hands. "Yet, you saved the lives of two people—Eric Gilmore and my brother."

Warmth worked through Chloe's face. *How right you are. I bet if Mark were alive, I wouldn't feel this crappy after donating stem cells.*

"The aches will pass." Althea patted her hand. "If you want, you can start over in my world."

Chloe jerked upright in bed. She opened her mouth to say yes, but another voice inside screamed, *Don't go! This house and the furnishings in it are all you've got left of Mark. How can you leave all that behind?*

"I don't know if Eric will survive," she responded instead. "I'd like to see how if my stem cells will help him."

"Staying will not affect the outcome." Moving a pillow, Althea sat beside Chloe, meeting her gaze intently. "Nothing's keeping you here."

Chloe lowered her gaze, plucking at the covers with despondent fingers. *Right again. Give the lady a balloon.* "Guess not."

"My people set up that portal so I can come here and search for the ones who've lost—or think they've lost—everything. Our doctors have advanced techniques to treat depression and other diseases. During the time of the ancient Egyptians, we lived among you, so we have similar body chemistry. We can ingest most things you do and vice versa.

"Once you've finish treatment, you take an aptitude test to place you in a job suited to your abilities. You then move into a community designed for humans. Androids would clean your living quarters and provide your meals."

Chloe gaped. "Popple Land would do that for me?"

"Popple Land?" Althea burst out laughing. "Is that what you call my world? I suppose the name will suffice, for now. We believe the good we do will come back to us. Karma."

Chloe chewed the offer over. She longed to escape Russell's tirades, the horror of watching her errors cause adverse symptoms, and her empty home. Life in Althea's world sounded great, but she suspected no aptitude test could explain her recent failures. "I need time to think about this. I'm so afraid my pattern would continue in Popple Land. No matter where I live, I'll always think of Mark."

"Are you sure?" Doubt edged into Althea's voice. "At least, you'd have a refuge."

"I need to work out my problems here, first. I appreciate your offer, and I may accept, in time. When I do, I want to do so with my head held high."

"Very well." Althea stood. "I wish you luck. Try to get some rest."

Moments later, the sound of high winds echoed from her living room. Getting up, she crept toward the doorway. Althea was gone. There was just the painting, this time showing Althea's side profile. A breeze stirred at Chloe's cheeks, then faded.

Something rubbed the back of her head. Chloe spun around in alarm. No one was there. A balloon had broken off the bouquet and drifted behind her. Smiling, she turned back toward the painting, the balloon rubbing her head with soothing strokes as if to say, *don't worry, everything will turn out all right.*

At the very least, it offered a distraction from her grief.

A distraction. That's the ticket. Her patients could use a distraction from their problems, too. Balloons would cheer them and take her mind off of Mark. Grabbing the balloon, Chloe hugged and kissed it. "I think you've given me a solution to my work problem."

****

Two weeks later

At the end of her shift, Chloe headed to her locker to retrieve the bouquet of rose-shaped balloons stored there, then made her way to Denise's office. She tapped on the door.

"Denise?" She held out the balloons and a gift card when her supervisor acknowledged her presence. "I want to thank you for looking after me when I had the stem cell infusion."

"Chloe, that was sweet of you." Denise opened the card, then gave her a tight hug. "I'll put the gift card to good use. Oh, and by the way, your patients are pleased with you. I hear you've been giving out balloons."

"Balloons cheer up people." Chloe smiled, thinking about Popple Land. It felt so good saving Althea's brother.

"Two of the nurses mentioned how hard you've been working."

"I'm trying. Does this mean I might be working on the critical floors again?"

"Not yet. You've only spent a month in therapy, and you're still making charting errors."

Wait until you hear about Popple Land's version of therapy. You'll love it.

"I wish I'd known about the way your mother-in-law hassled you." Denise shook her head. "That must have been awful for you."

Chloe gasped. Her arms jerked, scattering her papers on the floor. "Where did you hear that?"

"Eric. He told me she ruined your confidence."

"I see." Chloe crouched down to retrieve her sheets. "Where does he get his information? I haven't visited or spoken to Eric since you told me to stay away from him."

"That was Russell's order, but I think he may lighten up about that since you donated stem cells."

"Maybe." Chloe glanced through her assessment sheets before handing them to Denise. "How is Eric?"

"Why don't you ask him?" Denise grinned. "He wants to see you. By the way, who brought all those balloons to the house?"

"A neighbor. Apparently, people care more than I realize." Chloe smiled, but her heart pounded in dread at the thought of seeing Eric Gilmore again. She'd never forget the hate in his voice the day she messed up his blood test.

****

Donning her isolation gown and mask, Chloe shuffled into Eric Gilmore's room, to find him sitting up in bed, watching TV. Two needles were buried in his left elbow, one for platelets and the other for antibiotics. Chloe scanned his face, searching for rash or other sign of complications. None showed, except minimal paleness and cratered sores around his lips.

"Hello, Mr. Gilmore."

"Call me Eric. We're almost the same age." He smiled. "Have a seat."

After checking her gown's ties, Chloe pulled a chair to the bed. "Okay, Eric."

Eric's intent gaze made her fidget. Chloe leafed through the magazines on his table, hoping to find grist for conversation.

"Relax," Eric assured her. "I told Denise I wanted to see you."

"I know." Chloe swallowed hard. "How are you feeling?"

"I sleep a lot, and my mouth hurts. Doctor Williams said that should pass."

"She seems optimistic about your recovery." Chloe forced cheer into her voice. "I'm sorry for hurting you with the blood test."

"Your approach frightened me, but I owe you for donating the stem cells." Eric smiled. "What's a botched test when you saved my life?"

Chloe gasped. "That's confidential information. Doctor Williams wasn't supposed to tell anyone." She ran her trembling hands through her hair.

"She didn't. I overheard the nurses talking about it."

It figures. Another juicy tidbit for the Chloe Smythe Hate Club. "I just wanted to help. My husband died of a condition like yours."

"I know. He had leukemia, but he couldn't find a matching donor."

Chloe shook her head. Old resentment reared, and her hands shook. "I wish they'd kept quiet about that."

"Don't worry about it." Eric shrugged. "Sometimes I forget I'm not the only one with problems."

"That may be, but they committed a HIPAA violation." Chloe heaved a sigh. Her trembling eased. "At least, you're doing better."

Glancing at her watch, she rose stiffly from her seat. "I should go, but I'll stop by another time."

"Chloe," Eric called after her, "may I have a balloon?"

With a startled gasp, Chloe spun around. "What balloon?"

"The red Mylar balloons in your living room. A balloon might bring me luck." He grinned.

Red Mylar? I never told anyone about the balloons! Chloe froze, hand gripping the doorpost.

"Sure," she mumbled before skittering from the room.

****

One week later

Chloe spotted Eric in the transplant unit, riding a stationary bike. One hand behind her gowned back, fingers clutching a Mylar heart, she waved to him with her free hand.

"Hi!" Eric hopped off his bike, panting and glistening with sweat. He strolled into his room, Chloe behind him, and collapsed into his bed, gasping. "I should work on my conditioning."

"Give yourself time. You'll get there." Chloe managed a smile, then lifted the balloon from her gown's folds. "I've had this balloon two weeks, but it's still inflated. Enjoy."

"Holy..." Eric traced his finger along the designs. "It's covered with lace, just the way she..."

"Who, Eric?" Chloe shoved her hands into the gown's folds to still her quivering tension. "Doctor Williams? A nurse? Talk to me."

Eric's face turned crimson. "You wouldn't believe me."

"Try me." Chloe met his gaze resolutely.

"A woman wearing red visited me after my transplant. She looked like you, but pale, with yellow eyes. She called herself Althea and said she was your dimensional twin." He shook his head and regarded Chloe. "I'm sorry for rambling like this. All the drugs in my system probably caused me to hallucinate."

Chloe sank into a chair, bracing herself against the dizziness washing through her like a tidal wave. She leaned on his bed rail for support. "Did she tell you anything else?"

"Althea told me you donated the marrow. She said..." He shook his head. "You gave me a second chance at life, and it's a big deal because your mother-in-law harassed you after Mark died."

He shook his head again. "See? I'm not making sense. It's the drugs talking."

Chloe sat gaping, stunned to silence. *Of course, it's the drugs talking.*

If that's the case, you're both hallucinating. But you know differently. You know it's all true.

She cleared her throat nervously. "Maybe not. Tomorrow, I'm coming back because I'd like to show you a painting."

****

When Chloe picked up the *Popple Land* painting, it showed Althea and her brother walking the balloon-decorated street. The picture changed every day. Yesterday, the picture portrayed a deserted road.

After covering *Popple Land* with a sheet, Chloe placed it in the backseat of her car to bring to the hospital. She arrived after lunch, knowing Eric would be resting in his room.

"Take a good look at this painting." Chloe set *Popple Land* on the floor facing Eric, then yanked away the sheet. "Does any of this look familiar?"

"That's Althea." Eric pointed at the woman in the painting. "She's the one who told me about you."

"I see." The anxious tension knotting her muscles eased, and she smiled — probably her first genuine smile since Mark died. "I can't get mad at Althea for talking. She never worked at the hospital and didn't know the confidentiality policy. Besides, she was trying to help."

Eric drew in a sharp breath. "You *know* her? She's *real*?"

"She's visited me several times." Chloe explained how she became attracted to the *Popple Land* painting, how it changed every day since she brought it home; and her performing the life-saving Heimlich maneuver. "Has Althea suggested you move?"

Eric's face blanched, and he nodded. "She offered me a chance to start over where she lives. She said they have more advanced medicines and procedures. I hate being sick more than anything. I've used up all my sick time at my job, and my insurance benefits are shitty."

"And of course, Althea said those things wouldn't be a problem."

Another nod. "Exactly. Doctor Williams warned me I still have a chance of relapsing or I could get graft versus host disease."

Mark never mentioned these pitfalls. Was he trying to protect me? Chloe glanced at the painting as a breeze caressed her cheek. "But the decision isn't that simple. Your mother must be worried sick about you."

"You're right." Eric sighed. "My mom's taking this worse than I am. The other day, she called during my rest period. I was sound asleep, so I never heard the phone. She proceeded to call the nurses' desk and sent a nurse in here to make sure I was okay. She was in tears when we spoke. So now I call her every day before I take my nap."

I wish I had someone who worried about me like that. Chloe averted her gaze, blinking back tears. The breeze built up to a stiff wind. She shivered. "Maybe Althea would allow you to bring your mom along if you could convince your mom to go with you."

"Maybe." Eric furrowed his brows. "What's keeping you here?"

She longed to say, *My husband died, but I've got a bun in the oven, and my parents would miss both of us terribly.* It would be a lie, and what Eric needed was the truth. "Nothing."

"Nothing?"

"I don't have a family. You already know about Mark and his mother. My father died in a car accident when I was starting college, and I was an only child." She looked away. "My mother died of pneumonia the following year. That's why I became a respiratory therapist. I've had problems concentrating since Mark died, and I don't think running off to Popple Land will change that. I need to fix this before I make my decision."

"Popple Land?" Eric chuckled. "Is that what you call her world? I'm sure it comes with its own problems."

He shivered and hugged his blanket around his shoulders. "Hey, it's gotten chilly in here."

"I bet I know why." Rubbing her arms, Chloe glanced toward the painting, now enlarged to about half the size of the wall. Althea was moving. She grabbed several balloons off a tree and let them loose. The wind blew the balloons into Eric's hospital room. One bopped Chloe in the head, and another brushed Eric's shoulder.

The painting stilled, then reverted to its original size. The wind stopped. Eric burst into laughter. "What the heck was that all about?"

"That's a good question." Chloe smiled, hugging the balloon to her chest. "I think Althea's sending us another message about moving, and she wants a yes or a no."

"You think if we brainstorm, we can figure out an answer?"

"I think..." Chloe's smile grew. Impossibly, despite her early mistakes she'd made a friend in Eric Gilmore. "I'm willing to shoot for the moon."

Heather's Guiding Light

"You'd better hope Mr. Gaffney survives. If he doesn't, you're fired."

Heather Marsh sucked in a frightened breath at the threat in her boss's voice. The threat wasn't as unsettling as his thin-lipped frown or icy gaze. Those harsh gray eyes, above a coarse, jet beard, made Frank Rogan terrifying.

Heather's trembling fingers gave way around the cup of coffee she was drinking when summoned to Frank's office. The cup tumbled to his desk, spraying coffee over everything, including Frank's black business suit.

"I don't believe this." Frank blotted his clothes with a hanky. "Your patient exhibits classic signs of respiratory distress. Instead of turning up his oxygen or calling a doctor, you just stand there and watch."

Heather averted her face to hide the tears forming in her eyes. Mr. Gaffney's severe pneumonia left him gasping for every breath. The pleading in his eyes and cries for help would never leave her.

He reminded Heather of her father, who died a month ago. Her father suffered the same illness and symptoms that Mr. Gaffney did, right down to the irregular heartbeat, low oxygen saturation, and dusky, papery skin. Since her father's funeral, patient care at Wyman Hospital had become a daily reminder of his sickness and death.

"Cut the waterworks!" Frank's scowl darkened. "Thanks to your lack of action, Mr. Gaffney went into full-blown respiratory arrest and now requires a ventilator to breathe. His nurses tell me you just lost your father. Life goes on, Heather. A time comes when you have to move on. The Research Lab doesn't allow me time to accommodate your moods."

Heather balled her fists inside her pockets and gazed toward the door. She'd read about an extraterrestrial aircraft crashing into the Grand Canyon. According to her coworkers, the police found survivors and brought them to Wyman Hospital for treatment. *"Shit!"* a coworker said when she mentioned the crash. *"Frankipoo's probably using them for experiments."*

"Did we get any new patients in Research?"

"That's not your business." Brow furrowed in anger, Frank scribbled something on a notepad. "Just do your job. This memo will serve as a written warning. That could change, depending on the outcome of Mr. Gaffney's treatment."

"I'm sorry." Heather brushed back her auburn curls with trembling fingers. "I'll try harder."

"Trying won't cut it." Frank stood, jerking his thumb toward the hall. "I'm sending you home early to give you time to think about this. Tomorrow, when you come in, be ready to work. If you can't pull yourself together, there's the door."

Heather headed to her locker, head bent, breath hitching with sobs and tears running down her cheeks. She felt Frank's angry stare drill into her back, watching and waiting. After she got her purse and coat, she bolted to the exit, then down a flight of stairs to the parking lot where she parked her Honda Civic. Jamming her key into the ignition, she jarred her car into gear and sped from the lot.

A full moon shone overhead as she got on the road. Mill Road was shrouded in darkness as she turned off on the S-shaped road snaking through the woods Thanks to the terrible economy, the closest job she could get was an hour's trip from home.

Bright lights shone in her face, and she swerved her car, narrowly missing a tree. The lights faded after a moment, but Heather's fingers jittered against the wheel the rest of the drive home.

After a tense hour's drive, Heather shuffled into her three-room, ground-floor apartment and flopped onto her floral print sofa. Her gaze scanned the portraits she'd painted, including her father's, on the wall by the front door.

"If only Dad had allowed me to go to art school," she said aloud.

"Drawing won't pay the rent," he once told her, *"but an allied health career will always provide an income."*

Her father worked in construction and survived many layoffs, over the years. She knew he tried to spare her his pain, but the medical field didn't guarantee job security. Since Frank's hire, three of her coworkers quit, and two others were fired. Heather feared she'd go next.

"Oh, Daddy." Tears cascaded down her face. "Why did you leave me?"

Moments later, flashing lights outside illuminated her window. Heather dragged herself up from the sofa and peeped through her lace curtains. Glowing rays splayed along the streets—the same lights she saw in the woods. Her eyes shifted skyward.

"Holy shit!" Her eyes bulged. A bell-shaped object the size of a 747 loomed overhead. Shimmering lights studded its borders, bathing the apartments on her block in blues, greens, and violets.

Heather mopped sweat from her forehead. Troubles forgotten, she raced to her bedroom for her pad, pencils, and a paintbrush. "This should go on canvas."

Enthralled by the rainbow colors, she tiptoed out to her patio. The bright rays illuminated her block with an otherworldly glow. Her gaze never leaving the ship, she sketched and painted, trying to capture the dimensions and color effects. Perhaps someone was staging a light show or publicity stunt for a sci-fi movie.

Scraping footsteps jarred her attention away from her work just as two figures in cobalt blue suits and dome-shaped visors climbed over the patio railing.

Oh, my God, astronauts! Her paintbrush clattered to the pavement. Heather stared with widened, fearful eyes at her visitors. *Oh, my God, this is too much!*

A scream tore from her throat as she bolted for her patio door.

Too late.

Violet lights flared around her, freezing her in place, her scream trapped in her throat as the figures locked their arms under her shoulders.

An invisible force pulled at Heather, lifting her and her captors from her patio. The stiff October breeze whipped at her body, snapping her scrub pants against her legs. The ascent continued, and Heather fought waves of dizziness as her apartment building shrank into the distance below.

The lights faded, leaving Heather in some kind of conference room. Buttons with Greek-looking symbols studded the room's metallic gray walls. One of her captors motioned her to a chair. Heather sank into it gratefully, glad to be off her trembling legs.

The aliens removed their visors, showing ash-colored hair, canary yellow eyes, and humanoid features. Their smooth, albino skin made them look like ghosts. Would these ghosts harm her?

The female of the two paced around the table, meeting her gaze as she held up Heather's sketch pad. "What is this?"

Damn! I didn't see her take my pad. Still, the detail seemed far away and unimportant, while two aliens held her captive. She hugged herself, shivering.

"It's a painting of your ship. Your lights looked so beautiful, and I... I..."

"Picture?" The female spoke with a thick accent, but her accusation was loud and clear. "Who ordered you to do this?"

"Nobody. Painting... drawing is a hobby. Something I do for pleasure." Heather's voice hitched. "Please let me go."

"Go easy on her, Siduri." The male watched Heather intently. "She doesn't look dangerous."

"Doesn't she?" Siduri snapped. "Look at her uniform."

Uniform? Heather's teeth chattered. She cast a forlorn gaze at the maze of machinery, paneled walls, and grid floor.

"Look at her aura," the male countered. "She's terrified. She doesn't know what we are or why she's here."

"He's right." Heather shifted in her seat, rubbing her arms. Her gaze shifted between her two captors. Guns poked like mushrooms from their studded belts. A fresh tremble shuddered through Heather. *Oh, my God, they're going to shoot me!*

"If my drawing upset you, I'm sorry," she managed. "I never meant to cause any problems. Please don't hurt me."

"Heather, no one is going to hurt you." The male's voice was soothing and calm. "We carry weapons only for our protection."

Heather gasped. "How do you know my name?"

The male smiled. "You're wearing a plastic card that says 'Heather Marsh, R.C.P. What does 'R.C.P.' mean?"

"Respiratory Care Practitioner. I treat sick and injured people with lung problems." Heather pressed her fists against her trembling lips. "What should I call you?"

"Cronos." He pointed to the female. "My sister, Siduri. According to our surveillance, our father and his pilot crash-landed near your home, and we lost contact. Our search turned up the other passengers, who died, but no sign of my father or his pilot. At first, we thought Earth officials took them somewhere for treatment. However, neither our father nor his pilot, Endiku, contacted us, and it's been Earth weeks. We're afraid they either died or are being held against their will."

"Why did you come after me?"

"Siduri scanned you on our computer. Your uniform made you look like a government official." Cronos sighed. "We made a terrible mistake."

"Maybe not." Siduri's attention was fixed on the computer's view screen. "Our father could have gone to the center where Heather works."

The accident at the Grand Canyon. Heather's blood turned to icy with fear. She dragged shaking hands through her hair. "What are you people? Why would I have any contact with your father?"

"We live on Athyr—a planet in a galaxy light years from yours," Cronos explained. "Ours is an ancient civilization. We once lived among your Egyptians, thousands of years ago. Back then, our diets were similar. After we migrated, we continued to study your people. Your languages and customs intrigue us, but we can't understand why you have so many wars. Officials like our father continue to watch, hoping one day your people learn to settle their differences peacefully."

"I see." Alarms went off in Heather's head. "What happens if we don't live up to your expectations?"

"Nothing, so long as your people don't come after us." Siduri fingered Heather's name tag. "Wyman Hospital. What does 'hospital' mean?"

"It's a place where sick and injured people go for treatment." The chills settled around Heather's neck. "If the lungs are affected, then I work with them."

"A healer?" Cronos smiled, admiration edging into his voice. "Our society respects people like you."

"That's true." Siduri's voice softened. "If you are a healer, then you wouldn't hurt anyone intentionally, but humans can't read auras. You may work with our father's kidnapper without knowing it."

Heather's skin to gooseflesh as memories of Frank's "dumb-little-Heather" rants flashed through her.

"I hope not." She chewed anxiously on her thumbnail.

"Your drawing looks like our building plans." Siduri held the sketch to the light. "We've got computers that sketch the plans for our buildings and vehicles."

"Some humans make painting their profession." Heather bit her nail to the quick. "As I hope to some day."

Cronos pried her hand loose. "You're still frightened? Can't you see we're people, too? In many ways, we are like humans."

"I don't know what to think." Heather heaved a weary sigh. "I'm really sorry about your dad, but I don't know anything about his kidnapping. Why do you keep insisting I do?"

"Your aura says you're hiding something." A tear cruised down Siduri's porcelain cheek. "Whatever it is may provide a clue to help us save him."

Like I wanted to save mine. Heather blinked back tears. She recognized Siduri's pain in herself.

"However unimportant it may seem to you, the smallest detail may provide a clue." Cronos nodded encouragement.

"My father died of pneumonia last month," Heather admitted hesitantly. "So I understand your frustration. But I can't help you. Wyman Hospital doesn't keep prisoners, and even if they did, no one would tell me." Digging through her pockets, Heather grasped Frank's warning note. "If you can read this, you'll see the ones in charge wouldn't trust me with sensitive information."

"Our officials schooled us to speak, read, and write English." Siduri accepted the offered note. She spread it out on the table, with Cronos beside her. "It says that you failed to treat someone named Joseph Gaffney."

"I'm not proud of what I did." Heather closed her eyes against the memory. It didn't do any good. Opening her eyes, she looked back at the siblings. "Mr. Gaffney developed respiratory problems the way my father did before he died. His symptoms brought back painful memories and I froze."

"I've read grief can affect human behavior." Cronos lifted his gaze to hers. "You must have been close to your father."

Heather nodded. "I have no siblings and my mom died when I was ten years old. Now," her voice cracked. "I have no family."

"Your superior should have made allowances." Cronos scowled. "On our world, when an only child loses his parent, a neighbor will act as a surrogate. The surrogate treats the grieving person as if he were their own."

"Adoption?" Heather dabbed her eyes with a tissue. "People adopt children where I live, but it's a costly process and can involve many officials, depending on the country."

"We do it do verbally, without officials or exchange of funds. Your people would probably call it an informal agreement. But we consider it binding."

"I don't expect anyone to invite me to call them 'Dad' anytime soon. But I've sold some paintings. I think changing careers would help me feel better."

"Because you see so many clones of your father?" Siduri's hands cradled Heather's, feeling like satiny ice. "I should have recognized your sorrow, but I acted out of fear like you did with your patient. Can you understand that?"

Heather nodded, still thinking about Frank's glittering, hateful eyes and harsh voice. "Not knowing your father's whereabouts must be terrifying for you."

"That it is," Cronos agreed. "Tell us about your hospital."

"Wyman is a teaching hospital funded by the United States government." Heather paused, fearing she said something wrong, but their eyes registered compassion. "They've got a floor dedicated to developing new medicines and procedures. They experiment on mice before prescribing for humans. If the experiment goes well, they'll run clinical trials, meaning they try the new treatments out on a select group of people before releasing to the general market."

Siduri exchanged glances with her brother, tracing her tented fingers along the table. "That sounds intriguing."

Yeah, it's intriguing, all right. Heather covered her eyes, trying to blot out the memory of Frank's furious expression.

Cronos' eyes shone like amber lamps as he reached for her hands. "The man who wrote this message has frightened you for some time, hasn't he?"

Heather averted her gaze. "What makes you say that?"

"Your aura. Most life forms give off a glow that changes color according to their moods."

"Whatever you're hiding may prove vital to our search," Siduri said in a wistful voice. "I realize we frightened you, but since we have our love for our fathers in common, I hope you can tell us what you know."

Heather stared at Cronos and Siduri. Could she trust these people? Their concern for their father felt real. Memories of her father's suffering flashed through her mind. How would she feel if someone had kidnapped him?

"Okay, I'll tell you." Her voice softened. "According to our news, a ship like yours crash-landed into the Grand Canyon. My coworkers say the police found survivors and brought them to our research floor for experiments. My supervisor, Frank Rogan, runs that floor."

She paused, exhaling deeply. "Frank makes our lives miserable. He fired—terminated—several positions. Sometimes my coworkers make up stories about him to ease the tension."

"Maybe not this time." A deep sigh rolled from Siduri. "We should search Wyman's laboratory, Cronos."

"Heather can tell us where this laboratory is and how to get in." Cronos turned toward Heather. "Will you?"

Sweat dripped down Heather's forehead. She knuckled it aside with the back of her hand. "Of course, but I sure hope your father and pilot aren't at Wyman Hospital since Frank runs the research floor. So I'll look around the lab after my shift ends tomorrow night."

"That sounds reasonable." Cronos nodded. "We appreciate this."

Siduri pushed two buttons by a view screen. A sliding door above them opened, revealing a pink crystal.

"Carry this." She placed it into Heather's hand. "It contains a miniature camera which will enable us to track your movements. We'll find you after you've completed your mission."

Heather fingered the crystal. "It looks like a precious stone."

Smiling, she slipped it into her pocket. "Now that we're on the same team, may I finish my drawing?"

"I'd rather you didn't." Siduri handed her the sketchbook, minus her painting. "If you publicized any photographs or drawings of our ship, it may cause problems for us." She cut a glance toward her brother. "Cronos, let's take Heather back to her home."

Heather followed them down a flight of stairs. The two linked their arms around hers. Seconds later, a panel opened in the floor. A stiff breeze whipped at Heather as they drifted downward. This time, Heather squeezed her eyes shut.

Moments later, she stood alone in her patio.

Weariness settled over Heather. She glanced at her watch. It was almost 2:00 a.m. Yawning and rubbing her eyes, she trudged into her apartment. She crawled into bed still in her scrubs, and let oblivion wade in.

****

Heather woke to sunlight casting misshapen shadows on the walls of her bedroom. She still had on her pink scrubs. Something hard pressed against her hip when she rolled over in bed. Reaching into her pocket, she retrieved the object. As she stared down at the pink stone, last night's events rushed over her. It wasn't a dream, after all. The Athyrians gave her a job and would expect results.

She massaged her temples. "Oh, Heather, what have you gotten yourself into, now?"

Sighing, she headed to the kitchen for breakfast, then showered and changed into fresh scrubs. She turned on the TV to watch the news, but her mind kept straying back to the crystal—and the Athyrians' request.

When she glanced up at the clock, it was almost noon. Soon, she'd have to leave for work, since her shift began at three. She had just enough time to get lunch.

****

After lunch, she headed to work. She proceeded to the conference room for her shift report. While gathering her assignment sheets, she heard muffled footsteps from the hall, before a massive hand clapped her shoulder.

"Yikes!" Heather whirled around.

Frank towered over her, bearded lips curled into a malicious smirk and his gray eyes glittering like tarnished silver.

"The nurse manager spoke with me today." His voice dripped with condescension. "She suggested I assign you to floor care until you... how did she put it? Oh, yes, she thought you needed time to process."

"The manager and two of the nurses sat with me when my father died. Mr. Gaffney reminds me of my father. That's why I froze."

"Personally, I don't give a damn." Frank shoved a stack of flow sheets at her. "If I assigned everyone according to their problems at home, no one would work certain floors. So you'll work ICU, and I better not hear a repeat performance of last night."

Heather's fists clenched inside her pockets. "Maybe the nurse manager had a point."

Frank's eyes narrowed. "What did you say?"

"I said, I'm on my way." Shivering, she hugged her sheets to her chest and scurried to her assigned floor.

In the unit, Heather headed to Gaffney's room first. He still breathed on a ventilator. His silver hair and pale skin shone with sweat, and his dusky complexion reminded her of how her father's was the day before his death. Two older women sat by his side, hugging each other and weeping. After exchanging greetings, Heather checked his ventilator.

Seconds later, Gaffney's monitor sounded an alarm. His heart rate shot up, and his oxygen plummeted to 50% saturation. Foamy secretions bubbled inside his breathing tube. Heather turned up his oxygen and suctioned copious mucus plugs from his tube. His heart rate stabilized and the oxygen saturation returned to the 90s. Heather left the room blotting her eyes, her breath hitching with noiseless sobs.

****

Bad as the evening was, she was mindful of her mission. Thankfully, she made it through the rest of her shift without further incidents.

After her shift report, Heather drove to the rear gate and parked behind the ambulances. Entering the building, she took the service elevator to the eighth floor—Wyman's research floor. Right outside the elevator was an unmanned desk. The door behind it bore a sign reading, *Authorized Personnel Only*.

She tried the door's handle, before realizing it was secured by a combination lock. After trying several unsuccessful combinations, Heather cursed under her breath and scanned the hall, wondering where to find the right combination.

Muffled footsteps echoed down the corridor, heading her way. Heart hammering in fear, she ducked behind a gurney and waited. Moments later, the source of those footsteps came into view, wearing a bright blue hazmat suit. The suit's glass visor showed a woman's face, as the figure passed by Heather and went to the locked door. The woman pushed the two top buttons and two bottom ones on the keypad and went inside. Heather waited ten minutes, then used the same combination to open the door.

The doorway led to an anteroom facing a laboratory. Spotting a rack of hazmat suits, Heather grabbed one, skittered into the dressing room, donned the suit, and crept into the main laboratory.

Inside, cages of mice covered the wall to her right, and cubicles with glass doors stretched along the left wall, labeled alphabetically. Each door held a familiar metal disc. When she underwent her orientation tour after being hired, the guide told Heather these cubicles were for quarantined patients, and the discs were intercoms for the doctors and patients to communicate.

A deep groan issued from inside Cubicle A, where a man writhed against leather ties. His dusky complexion contrasted with the shiny amber of his eyes. Intravenous needles wedged into his neck leaked black, filmy fluid.

Heather gasped. *He must be Cronos and Siduri's father.*

Keeping her head low, she tiptoed toward Cubicle A, even as she realized the Athyrian siblings hadn't told her their father's name.

"Father?" She tapped on the glass.

The man's gaze flickered her way, but he didn't answer.

"Father," she tried again, raising her voice a notch. "Siduri and Cronos are looking for you."

"Siduri and..." Disbelief darkened his amber gaze. "Who are you?"

"I'm Heather. I'm... a friend." Heather swallowed hard. Why hadn't she thought to ask them his name? She darted a glance around the laboratory.

"How do you know my children?"

"It's complicated." Heather drew in a sharp breath. "Cronos and Siduri are terribly worried about you. I know what it's like to lose a father, so I promised to help. We're going to..." *bust you out of here,* her final words were cut off by the slam of a door, followed by footsteps.

"Excuse me," she whispered instead, darting into a utility closet.

Inside, she left the door ajar just a crack, so she could see what was happening in the lab. She couldn't see the Athyrian in Cubicle A anymore, but she could look into Cubicle B, which housed a female Athyrian attached to a ventilator.

Clad in hazmat suits, two men ambled inside, speaking in hushed tones. The glass visor of one man revealed Frank's thick beard and sadistic grin.

"Wake up, E.T." He brandished a syringe, its needle gleaming in the light. "I've got to take blood."

Cubicle B's occupant thrashed against her restraints as the needle punctured her skin.

"Whoops, I missed. Here we go again." Frank whispered something to his companion, and they exploded with laughter. "Last night, it took me eight tries to get her blood."

Copious liquid seeped from her breathing tube. From where she hid, Heather made out the woman's grunting respirations.

"Oh, well." Frank's partner chuckled. "We turn in our report, we get rich."

"You've got that right." Blood sample in hand, Frank swaggered down the hall. "Let's beat it."

After the men left, Heather bolted from the lab without bothering to change her suit. She sprinted down the stairs to the rear exit and the lot where she parked her Honda. Inside the car, she sat panting for breath, when she heard urgent tapping on her window.

Afraid she was busted, Heather jerked her head up. Relief plunged through her to see Cronos and Siduri. Opening a door, she watched as they sprawled into the backseat.

"What are they doing to him?" Siduri's voice bled with urgency.

"Frank locked your father and another Athyrian in glass cubicles," Heather managed between rugged breaths. "Your father's alive, but he's hurt. His companion's in critical condition—she needs a ventilator to breathe. What's more, Frank's been torturing her—stuck her eight times to get blood, then bragged about it."

"That must be Endiku," Cronos said.

"We can save her," Siduri responded. "Your Frank sounds like a cruel person."

Heather nodded stoically. "And dangerous."

"How do we get into your laboratory?" Cronos's tone was no-nonsense.

"Your suits and my hazmat suit are almost the same color, so I could get you into the lab without any problems. I don't know how to open the cubicle doors, but I doubt they'd be an issue for you."

"No, they wouldn't," Siduri agreed. "How many people work in that laboratory?"

"Too many." Heather rubbed her arms, shivering. "If you're planning a rescue, we can move your father and pilot out on gurneys—portable beds. Loading them into the ambulance—what we use to transport the sick—would be best. If we have to move quickly, we could use my car, but I don't have room for two injured people."

Cronos' eyes widened. "What you're proposing will put you in danger."

"Tell me something I don't know." Heather's lips trembled, but she met Cronos' gaze resolutely. "I can't turn a blind eye to Frank's brutality. I'll help in any way I can."

Siduri and Cronos exchanged glances before Siduri spoke. "Your aura alone speaks of sincerity. How can we make the way easier for you?"

"You'll need a portable ventilator for your pilot, and medical supplies."

Cronos unbuckled the huge backpack he wore. "Our camera showed Endiku on a ventilator, so I've brought one, and other supplies. Anything else?"

"I don't have keys to open the ambulance door or start the vehicle. We'll probably set off alarms, and I don't know how to silence them."

"Not a problem," Siduri assured her. "You've got our protection. Lead the way."

With the Athyrians behind her, Heather headed for the stairwell this time. Stairs meant fewer chances of getting caught. The climb to the eighth floor was brutal in the heavy hazmat suit, and she was drenched with sweat when they arrived, but the lack of confrontation was worth it. At the locked stairwell door, she scanned her badge against the mechanical eye, unlocking their way in. To her surprise, the door opened into the laboratory itself. Holding a finger to her lips, she waved the Athyrians into the apparently unoccupied room, except for the mice and patients.

The Athyrian suits are a darker shade of blue, but the difference is hardly noticeable. If we proceed quietly, this might work. Maybe. Fear of discovery pumped adrenaline through Heather's body. Any moment, Frank or one of his buddies could show up.

Siduri let out a cry, burst into tears, and scurried to Cubicle A. Her fingers darted over the keypad above the disc, and the glass window opened like a coffin lid, giving her access to bend over the occupant, whispering and weeping.

Cronos shuffled toward Cubicle B. "Endiku looks worse than I saw on camera. Those needle marks on her are infected. This will be difficult."

"Are you saying she's going to die, despite your technology?"

"Not necessarily, but moving her safely will be difficult."

"I see." Drawing in a sharp breath, Heather rolled a stretcher toward Cubicle A. "I'll stand lookout while you transfer your dad to the gurney. Then we can load him on the ambulance. We'll need one for Endiku, too. The service elevator is wide enough; I think we can all fit."

"Right. Let's go, Siduri." Cronos opened the glass window for Cubicle B.

Siduri straightened, shaking her head. "We'll have to make two transfers. Endiku needs too much monitoring equipment. And if any officers show up..."

"All right." Cronos' lips puckered, his expression thoughtful. "We'll move Father first, and come back for Endiku. But we may not get the opportunity again once the people who manage this laboratory realize Father is missing. We may have to go without her."

Heather stood watching the door while Cronos and Siduri lifted their father onto the stretcher. So far, no footsteps or movement outside the door. Then again, the activity behind her provided too much background noise to hear. She was about to warn her companions to quiet down when the door burst open. The intruder's visor showed a woman's beet-red face and blonde hair.

"What's going on?" she demanded.

Heather glanced toward Cubicle A. "I'm transferring specimen A to another facility."

"I get all incoming orders." The woman's thin-lipped frown deepened. "No one said anything about moving the specimens."

Heather mustered her therapist's voice, hoping her panic wouldn't bleed through. "I took the call because you weren't at your desk."

"I only... wait a minute." The woman's eyes narrowed. "You don't work here."

"No, she doesn't." Frank's harsh voice bellowed from the doorway. Eyes glittering like bloodstones, he drew a revolver from his pocket. "As it is, she's on probation."

Heather opened her mouth, but the shrill bray of alarms from outside cut her off.

"Your so-called *specimen* has a family," she shouted over the alarms. "They've come to take him home. Let them go."

"Shut up!" Frank brandished his gun, finger cocked against the trigger. "You'll just..."

Violet rays shot across the room, circling Frank. His voice faded and he froze, gun still aimed at Heather.

"My laser will only stun him temporarily," Cronos nudged her toward the door. "Go!"

"It's too late." Heather steered the gurney toward the elevator, with the Athyrians flanking her. "That alarm will alert government officers and soldiers. I'm as good as dead."

"You don't know that."

Footsteps echoed from the stairwell. The door flew open, revealing men in blue uniforms. They charged toward Heather and her companions. "Freeze!"

"Get on the elevator." Siduri pushed her through the doors. "We'll handle this."

Several skin-slapping explosions followed. Heather ducked, narrowing missing the bullets slamming into the elevator walls. Another blast, then silence. Siduri and Cronos fired their stun lasers as Heather loaded the gurney onto the elevator. They backed into the elevator behind her, and the doors closed.

As soon as the elevator doors opened on the ground floor, Heather sprinted toward the parking lot with the Athyrians and their cargo behind her.

"Cronos, open the door to one of those trucks," Siduri ordered. "I'll load Father into the back."

Heather darted a gaze from the Athyrians to the hospital. The alarms were still deafening. "Siduri, no. We don't have time to break into the trucks."

Cronos hesitated, his gaze shifting between the building and Heather and Siduri. "She's right. Heather, can you use your vehicle?"

"I can if I lay the passenger seat flat for Father." *Oh, great, now I'm talking like he's my dad and I'm their sibling. Oh, well.* "I'll drive, but you two will have to sit close together in the back." Noting Siduri's crestfallen expression, she added, "I have a couple of blankets on the backseat to make your father comfortable."

"We do what we must," Cronos told his sister. "Let's move."

The transferring went slower than Heather would have liked. She laid the front passenger seat flat. Cronos and Siduri's father groaned with every movement as he was lifted into the seat. Heather hopped into the driver's seat while the others squeezed into the back.

Too late.

Heather's heart plummeted at the sight of officers spilling out into the parking lot. However, before the officers could aim their weapons, Siduri and Cronos opened the windows and fired the numbing lasers.

The windows shut. Siduri hollered, "Heather, go!"

Good thing traffic is light. Heather keyed the engine, even as she caught sight of movement in the rearview mirror. More officers. Jamming her foot down on the accelerator, she sped onto the street in a cloud of blue smoke, only dimly aware of the gunfire behind her.

Sirens wailed, and Heather picked up speed, zig-zagging through a labyrinth of intersections. She zipped through a lot, brushing a fruit stand. Oranges, apples, and other fruit spilled onto the ground in her wake. The officers slowed, giving her an advantage. She whipped up a side street, making sure she lost her pursuers before heading out to a wooded area. "Where should I take you?"

"The woods will do." Siduri pointed to a thick grove of trees. "Take a left up the path and drive as far as you can."

Moments later, the path narrowed to the size of a walkway. Heather stopped. She reached for the door, but Siduri stayed her hand. "Wait. We shall go up together."

Go up where? Heather arched one eyebrow in question.

Lights bathed the car in yellow and gold hues. Weightlessness seized Heather, lifting her, her companions, their father and the car. Her mouth went dry and perspiration bathed her body. What could generate a force strong enough to lift four people inside a car?

Aboard the ship, she found herself parked alongside other vehicles. Siduri and Cronos left the car and lifted Father. With Heather's help, they got onto a lift to the conference floor. Siduri and Cronos removed the intravenous needles, replacing them with IV equipment and medicine from their ship. Heather watched, weeping silently as she thought of her father. She wished he was alive so she could tell him about Frank, and meeting people from another world.

"What's wrong?" Siduri asked after they had finished their ministrations.

"Frank had no right to do this." Heather could barely contain her rage. "If my father were alive, he would have been horrified. Not all of us are like him."

"We know." Turning toward Heather, Cronos draped his arm across her shoulder. "Your father sounds like he was a fine man."

"He was." Heather looked up at Cronos and thought, *I wish I could have met you guys under peaceful circumstances. I bet you've got quite a story to tell.*

"Your influence gives me hope for your people." The man from Cubicle A opened his eyes and turned his head toward Heather. "But sending you home now would ensure your death. I can't allow that."

"Father!" Heather rushed to his side. "Are you going to be all right?"

The man nodded and smiled, fine wrinkles dimpling his chin. "My people heal fast. I'll live, and so will you. Endiku and I planned to study your solar system during the next six Earth months. Stay with us, Heather. By the time we finish, your police will tire of looking for you."

Heather's eyes widened. "What happens then?"

"We'll let you off anywhere you wish. You can start a new life."

"Thank you, Father!" Heather smiled through her tears. "I'm sorry... What should I call you?"

"'Father' will do nicely." He clasped her hand in a firm grip.

A Promise to Keep

Whistling alarms startle me awake to the sight of glass walls all around me. Leather restraints chafe my arms. The respirator pumping air into my chest makes a whirring sound — *wheeze-treat, wheeze-treat*. Something must have gone awry with my breathing and set off the alarms. My cardiac monitor flashes bright number — red for heart rate and white for oxygen saturation — and blue hoses tug at my lips. With a sick feeling, I remember I've spent the past Earth-standard months in Wyman Hospital's research laboratory — a prisoner used for experiments.

"Death," I mouth in my native tongue, listening to the erratic beep of my heart. My lips form words, but my voice is truncated by the hard pressure of the plastic breathing tube blocking all sound from leaving my mouth. Because I am female, my airway is narrow, making this tube particularly uncomfortable. Indeed, pain is a constant companion, reminding me that I am a prisoner.

The monitor beeps as the oxygen saturation drops again. The chemicals flowing through my veins burn my limbs like acid. As an Athyr pilot who studied Earth medicine, I know my body can't tolerate most human drugs. I tried to explain this to Doctor Rogan. He just smiled and continued to ply me with more medicines.

His partner, Doctor Kilroy, set up a computer at my footboard to observe virtual reality's effects on my kind. Sometimes, the screen immerses me in a cratered world — a desert inhabited by prehistoric monsters, the sensation of wind blowing around me, and the smell of sand. Other times, I find myself in a garden, inhaling the sweet scent of exotic flowers. The distractions are temporary. Nightmares haunt my sleep, and I grow weaker with every passing day.

"Life." A silvery voice whispers near me. I turn my head slowly, having learned that that quick movements would cause my breathing tube to shift painfully, but eager to make eye contact with the speaker.

Most laboratory personnel wear pressurized isolation suits, but my visitor — a blonde female-- wears a pink dress and shoes with spiked heels. Her black overcast aura indicates death. The soil-encrusted lacerations on her cheeks give off a purulent odor. Her mournful green eyes whisper of lethal assault. She looks like the nurse manager who was on duty at the laboratory not long ago.

Without so much as a wince or groan, she hobbles up the steps into my cubicle. The hem of her dress flaps around the purpling bruises on her calves. A scream dies in my throat as panic assaults me. She's here to kill me. I thrash against my ties, setting off another chorus of alarms.

"I'm sorry. I didn't mean to frighten you, Endi-ku." A marble-cold hand brushes against my arm. "I came here to help. If you think out your questions, I'll understand you."

Get out! I think between gagging coughs. *Go home!*

"I can't." A tear rolls down her left cheek. "Rogan made my leaving impossible."

How can Rogan stop someone from leaving? How is she able to read thoughts?

Then again, nothing about Rogan would surprise me. Last time he took my blood, he wore a malignant grin the whole time he was jabbing my arm like a piece of meat.

Did he? I glare at her, fearful and angry. *My ship crashed into your Grand Canyon. Only two of us survived. Rogan insists on poisoning me with your drugs and you went along with him.*

"Rogan was my boss." The woman gazes at my intravenous pumps. "Does he know these drugs are poisonous?"

I nod. Rogan laughed off my protests when I told him about the drugs. None of the staff have ever acknowledged my attempts to communicate. I belong to a foreign world, so they treat me as an experimental animal.

My chest tightens, and black, filmy secretions bubble through my breathing tube. My respirator whistles, and the buzzing monitor broadcasts my poverty of oxygen.

My visitor fades into the shadows, and a man wearing a white pressurized suit bursts into my cubicle. A handgun pokes from his side pocket. His glass visor reveals ice-gray eyes above a thick, black beard. Frank Rogan. The director of Wyman's Research Laboratory.

"What's wrong?" He croons, aspirating the secretions while I gag on the stink of distilled liquor coming off him. Though thick blankets covered me, chills wrack my body and tears flood my vision.

"Why the waterworks?" His voice reeks of contempt. "Kilroy should have snowed you."

Why would he want to cover someone with snow? Clearly, he means it in a way I don't understand. It doesn't matter. Rogan's sadistic smile warns me he plans more excruciating procedures.

"See what you're doing for mankind?" He's talking as if I answered him. "One day, you'll make me rich."

Without waiting for a reaction, he turns on his heel and marches out the doors.

Sick with pain and despair, I stare at the cages of mice along the wall opposite my cubicle. I know exactly how they feel.

Who paid Rogan to torture me? What about humanity? Closing my eyes, I focus on what I can remember of my life before imprisonment.

My home planet, Athyr, evolved over millions of years. My people once looked human; but evolution gifted us with smooth, albino skin, yellow eyes, and a pointed chin. Not to mention an average intelligence quotient over 200.

My government studies developing worlds, including Earth. Its languages intrigue us, but no one can understand why its history is littered with war. We planned to share our technology and resources, once humans learned to settle their differences peacefully.

In the meantime, the King decided to send delegates to chart Earth's progress. He chose Gyes to captain the last mission. Gyes chose me for his pilot. My ten years' experience with interstellar travel qualified me to handle the flight.

Even seasoned pilots can have accidents, though, and accidents in space can kill. Comets tore into our ship, and we smashed into Earth's canyon. In a smaller vehicle, I would have died on impact. As it was, everyone aboard perished except Gyes and me. My airway swelled from the fumes, shutting down my lungs and necessitating the ventilator now breathing for me.

Rogan and his team of scientists found the crash site. He promised he'd do everything to save Gyes and me, but his dark aura warned of lies. Still, I could only read auras. I couldn't figure out the details.

Gyes sustained blisters on his arms and chest, but he walked to the Wyman Hospital shuttle on his own. Weeks later, he was bedridden. Rogan said he developed an infection.

His explanation didn't make sense. The Athyr metabolism enables us to fight most germs. Maybe Gyes' injuries compromised his immune system. More likely, Rogan poisoned Gyes with his so-called therapies.

Last week, a native healer named Heather led two Athyrians through the laboratory. I recognized the visitors as Gyes' children, Siduri and Cronos. Both are experienced pilots. Heather helped them load Gyes onto a moving bed. They came toward my cubicle, but the nurse manager stopped them. Rogan burst through the doors with a gun and began shooting. His bullets flew across the laboratory, missing my would-be rescuers by a few centimeters. Only the gods know what happened after that. No one volunteered any information, and what questions I had resulted in cold, silent stares by my keepers.

"Don't worry. Gyes and his rescuers escaped." My current visitor stood by my computer.

I cough as I recognized my visitor. She was the nurse manager who stopped my rescue but hasn't shown up for work since Gyes' liberation. Fear and poverty of oxygen leaves me gasping. Another blast of alarms follows.

"I hate what Rogan's done to you." She blots my face with a damp towel. "In case you're wondering why I look the way I do, Rogan blamed me for Gyes' escape. He pistol-whipped me to death, consigning me to a cyber dimension where lost spirits roam before facing judgment. Apparently, some magnetic force between you and virtual reality forged a gate to the real world, so here I am." She meets my gaze directly. "As I said, you can think out your questions. People's minds, including those of extraterrestrials, have become open books to me."

You knew Rogan's experiments could kill, yet you tried to prevent Heather and the others from rescuing me. Why? Do you even care?

"More than you think." Her shoulders slump; she lowers her eyes. "I had to obey Rogan because my ten-year-old son has leukemia. Johnny needed my salary and health benefits to pay for his chemotherapy. When I died, my benefits stopped and so did his medicine. He's getting sicker now and will die soon without treatment."

Should I believe this stranger? Her dark gray aura radiates intense pain and self-loathing. Her intentions don't matter, though. I'm still going to die. *The maternal streak runs strong with most species. If you had told Gyes or me, we could have helped Johnny.*

"I wasn't thinking." The nurse manager's mournful eyes and quavering voice tell their own story. Rogan frightened her badly when she was alive. "Rogan made me an offer I couldn't refuse."

What offer? Who are you?

"Mary Westcott. Rogan reported me missing, but the police never found a body or any clues. Johnny figured out what happened. He's afraid Rogan will kill him next."

Gyes operates our Space and Cybernetics Agency. If he tells our King about Rogan, my government might declare war.

"I understand." Mary's voice cracks. She blinks back tears. "I'm sorry."

I avert my gaze, wishing she'd leave. She prevented my rescue, so her apology means nothing.

More charcoal secretions bubble from my mucus factory, rattling in my chest.

"Everyone's afraid of Rogan. Even Doctor Kilroy."

Kilroy's no better than Rogan. I cough again, setting off the ventilator alarm.

The cubicle glass panel slides open, admitting a scowling Rogan. An empty test tube rolls off the table and plops onto the floor. His foot lands on it, and in seconds he's on his buttocks.

Cursing, he scrambles back to his feet. He scowls at the floor. "Pigsty!"

"Pigsty." He tosses the test tube into a sharps container.

"Pigsty." He scoops dirty linen off the floor.

His repetitive behavior reminds me of a malfunctioning robot. I turn my head, hoping he won't notice my smile.

Fists clenched and eyes blazing, Rogan shoots me a withering glance. "I'll let you drown in your secretions. Then we'll see how much you laugh."

He limps back out to the hall.

My smile flees, chased by the burden of stagnant secretions. Whoever left the test tube on the floor signed my death warrant. I try to scan the room, but the computer blocks my view of the left side of the laboratory, its screen an eerie glow in the dim room.

Again, I find myself looking into a garden. Smoky wisps waft from the shadows. The smoke congeals into a human form until Mary is standing beside my bed again.

What are you doing? I cough again. *People can't travel through virtual reality.*

"Maybe not as flesh and blood, but after death, their spirits can. Other humans can't see them." Mary heaves a sigh. "I caused Rogan's fall because he upsets you. He deserves a taste of his poison."

Her expression softens. "I can get you the right medicine, but I'd have to label it so that he wouldn't notice. That's easy because I know my way around this laboratory and its computers. Will you let me help you?"

Dare I trust this stranger? Under normal circumstances, I would scream for help. However, her sorrow seems genuine. I don't know if I can believe her, but my diminishing oxygen stores leave me no choice. *Please do.*

After Mary clears my secretions, she checks my flow chart. "Rogan prescribed Gentamicin and Dopamine. Which do I stop?"

Both. Gentamicin burns my skin and veins. The blood pressure runs low in Athyrians, so giving me Dopamine could cause a stroke. Why are you going to this trouble?

"Because we're both Rogan's victims. The doctors here develop new medicines to treat incurable diseases. Most test the drugs on mice before administering to humans, but Rogan never follows the protocol. He jokes with the patients and nurses, but his eyes don't smile."

Her voice cracks. "The night he brought you and your friend here, he said, 'Mary, you've got a nice son. Keep it that way.'"

I've seen Rogan's slick demeanor when dealing with public dignitaries. No one reported his shooting spree. Instead, his superiors praised him for saving the hospital money.

Rogan never discusses his personal life. I suspect he guards his secrets well. *One day, Mary, your police will catch him.*

"That won't happen. He bribes too many people." Mary's fear and pain are palpable in the room." Know the worst part? My boy lost his father. He's an orphan now, and without my insurance to pay for treatment, he'll die from his leukemia — alone."

Her gaze turns toward the hallway. "Gyes cried for help, but I didn't listen. When your condition deteriorated, I still failed to pay attention. But I wised up when Rogan and his goons shot at Heather and your friends."

She pauses, drawing a breath to compose herself. "After the shooting, I told Rogan to find someone else to guard your cubicle. He smiled and said, 'Okay, Mary.' That night, as I walked to my car, he grabbed me and beat me until I lost consciousness. I can't rest because I've got unfinished business involving you and Johnny."

Anger and sorrow swirl through me, causing my hands to tremble. Anger for being on the ventilator, and sorrow over Mary's death and her son's illness. *If only you'd come to me in the beginning, I could have helped your son. Now I can't, given my current condition.*

"Maybe I can undo the damage Rogan has done."

I doubt it. Rogan makes all the decisions about my treatment.

"Not all. Rogan's mean when he drinks, and Kilroy doesn't like that. After my death, I saw Rogan as a boy, repeatedly burned with cigarette butts and hot irons by his father. Something broke inside him, so he beat up his wife. She left. Now, he attacks patients and staff. One nurse complained to Kilroy about him." She nods as if confirming this to herself. "Kilroy listened."

I shut my eyes and contemplate the past weeks. I remember Kilroy watching while Rogan performed a blood test. When Rogan boasted how he stuck me eight times, Kilroy laughed and said they would get rich anyway. *You think so? Kilroy laughs when Rogan hurts me.*

"Kilroy laughs with Rogan to humor him." Mary's measured, quiet voice is strangely soothing. "Humans often fake emotions to avoid confrontations. After the shooting, Kilroy told Rogan he didn't want bloodshed."

I find that hard to believe. Still, Rogan orders the most painful procedures and toxic drugs, not Kilroy. One night, Rogan wore tinted glasses under his visor, and he spoke in a high-pitched, agitated voice. I remember a nurse asking him if he was feeling sick.

Rogan said he caught a virus. His set jaw, glittering eyes, and condescending tone discouraged further questions at the time.

Gyes' children came to save their father. Had the gods not watched over them, Rogan's bullets would have killed Gyes, his children, and the young lady with them. Rage wells up inside me, and I know now what I have to do. I have to get better and warn my people. Rogan has declared war, and we must retaliate.

I'm shoving my way up out of bed, barely aware of the impossibility of such an action until I realize my limbs are smoky wisps. Standing by Mary, I hardly recognize the emaciated figure covered with plastic tubes as my body. My pale, sore-encrusted face shines with sweat, and the cardiac monitor continues to beep.

Oh, no, this can't be happening! I glance toward the lush scenery in the virtual world, wondering whether I should run. *I'm not ready to die.*

"You're not dead," Mary assures me. "You're having an out-of-body experience."

That's not possible. One may conjure their image by hologram, but their soul never leaves the body.

"Maybe not on Athyr," she agrees, "but you can't predict how your body will react to external stimuli like virtual reality. When you're this sick, spirit travel is easy. Relax and let yourself float."

I drift toward the computer. *Maybe I can travel through this virtual world.*

"I wouldn't try," Mary advises. "You'd sever the link with your body since only the dead can travel. What's more, evil spirits roam in the virtual world."

Oh, no! I recoil several paces. *Your world is filled with lethal traps. Rogan merely has to push a button, and I'm dead.*

"Unless something happens to him." Mary smiles.

Rogan isn't the only one. I stare at my ghostly limbs. How is it Mary and I can communicate? I guess it no longer matters, since we were spirits now. No one can overhear us. *His nurses do everything he tells them. They never explain procedures or ask how I'm feeling.*

"I'll look after you." Mary's steady eye contact speaks volumes. She leans closer to me. "If you give me the formula, I'll concoct any IV medicine you need, but label the bag so Rogan doesn't notice."

I sigh. *Mary, I appreciate this more than I can tell you, but Rogan isn't stupid. He'll figure out what you've done after he notices my improvement.*

Mary's started toward the computer. "Not if you tell Kilroy what Rogan did to us. Kilroy loves money, but he hates violence. He'll listen if you tell him where the police can find my body. It's buried under an oak tree, in a cemetery off Sunset Road."

Under an oak tree. Cemetery just off Sunset Road. All right, I'll tell him. But Kilroy may repeat what I say to Rogan and get me killed.

"Ah, but administrators can have accidents. It can happen if you spirit-travel around them." Mary's lips tip up in a conspiratorial smile. "The demons in the virtual world hunger for flesh. Any spiritual essence will open a gate between the virtual world and reality, with disastrous results around humans."

A being with a skull face shambles from behind a fruit tree in the virtual garden. Its mouth is open wide, displaying teeth shaped like battered tombstones. It growls as its dark, pitted eyes settle on me. I cringe. Mary backs away, waving me toward the bed.

"Look. I'll put together your formulas, but I need a favor, too."

Very well. No IV antibiotics, except penicillin for the infection in my lungs. Instead of antibiotic ointment, use tylotoin ointment for the sores on my skin. The isotonic sodium chloride that you use to hydrate patients should work for me. I then gave her the doses and had her repeat each medicine and dose back, so I knew she had it right. *What is the favor?*

"Go visit my Johnny and cure him. I'll give you his address. He lives with my sister, not far from this hospital."

Would he accept my help? Would your sister let me into her home? Most humans fear people like me.

"Not Johnny. He wants to become an astronaut. He's been following the Grand Canyon accident on television. He and my sister are desperate for a cure and will gladly accept any help they can get. Tell them Momsy worked with you in the lab. He used to call me Momsy during his playful moods before cancer ruined everything."

If I survive, I promise to do everything I can to ensure a full recovery for Johnny.

Mary heads toward the exit. "You should return to your body now. I have some formulas to prepare."

I float toward my bed. Cotton sheets press against my back, and the ventilator pumps air through the thick tube wedged in my throat. Drowsiness overtakes me and the oblivion of sleep sets in.

****

After an indeterminate amount of time, two nurses come to change my dressings and linens. They move like robots, never speaking or smiling. The porthole windows of my cubicle reveal an azure sky, but I can't tell whether it is morning or afternoon, let alone what day it is. My clock shattered during the crash, and without it, I can't tell time.

Doctor Kilroy steps into my cubicle as the nurses leave. He darts a glance over his shoulder before sliding the door shut. His hands quiver and he drops his papers.

"Clumsy me!" He chuckles, but his voice edges with tension. A gray-tinged aura of fear cloaks him.

"Your condition shows improvement." He straightens from retrieving his papers. "You still have some fever, but your oxygen levels have improved."

I indicate my understanding with a nod. I would thank him if I could talk.

"I have some bad news, though." Kilroy draws in a sharp breath. "Last night, a nurse on this floor was found unconscious, bludgeoned by a metal instrument. No one admits to seeing anything. She's in a coma."

Rogan again! Liquid terror burns through my veins, followed by another explosive cough.

"Easy." Kilroy's voice quavers with tension. "Slow down your breathing."

I turn my face in the direction of the monitors, but Kilroy's lean frame blocks my view. Several minutes passed before he spoke again.

"That's better." He sighs. "The police suspect last night's assault was related to a disappearance last week. They want to question the staff and patients. I told them I would evaluate the patients up here first before allowing any interrogation."

Another deep breath." I understand your people can read auras. That speaks of hyper-vigilance, and I suspect being attentive enabled your friend to escape. So I'd like to hear your observations."

He paces the room, eyeballing my monitors. "Given the seriousness of your condition, I hate coming at you with questions, but I find these crimes worrisome because there's been no sign of a break-in."

Why is he coming to me with this? Desperation and fear, judging by his muddy aura and tight-lipped frown. A scream worked through my chest, though the breathing tube made screaming impossible.

Kilroy paces around my bed, Teflon-sleeved arms cradling his papers, eyes on my monitors. "Another thing. Frank explained how the drugs intended for humans affect your species differently, and he factored this into your treatment plan. Still, you continue to have serious complications."

I shrug, not daring to volunteer information.

Kilroy withdraws a plastic sheet full of English letters and numbers from his pile. Untying my hands, he hands me the sheet.

"I assume you can read English. Invasive procedures aside, how would you describe a typical day? How do Rogan and his nurses treat you? Don't look at me like that. I want you alive and healthy. Your knowledge can help my world. One day, you'll return to Athyr. So talk to me."

I inspect my hands. My arms are swollen and ache terribly. Pointing with my forefinger, I spell out the answer. *You won't believe me.*

Kilroy meets my gaze, his resolute as steel. "Try me."

The tightness flares in my chest again, warning me any more excitement could offset the gains I've made. I have to make every word count. *No one introduces themselves or asks how I feel. Rogan's medicines are making me worse, and when I complain about them, he gets angry.*

"Frank Rogan?" Kilroy's dark brows furrowed. "He can be temperamental sometimes. His techniques are irregular, but he's respected for his knowledge. Are you sure?"

Quite sure. He pistol-whipped Mary Westcott, your nurse manager. You'll find her body under an oak tree in a cemetery off Sunset Road.

Kilroy's cheeks turn drywall white as a gasp explodes from him. "Do you realize what you're saying? Where did you get your information?"

I raise my hand to point, but a vicious cough seizes me, setting off more alarms. Starving for air, I clutch my chest.

Kilroy glances at the monitors. "You've had enough. I'll order a light sedative to help you sleep."

In other words, he didn't believe me. Whenever my behavior offends a staff person, the doctors order a sedative. Gyes received the same treatment. I never understood why. I look away while Kilroy ties my hands.

****

As time wears on, I sleep. My body has confused days with nights. Without my clock, I can't tell Athyr time from Earth time, or when I might expect my next round of medicines. When I open my eyes again, darkness surrounds me. A deathly silence hangs in the air, broken only by the ventilator's hum and the beeping monitor.

Moments later, clicking footsteps jar me to attention. The door to my cubicle opens. An overhead light snaps on, illuminating Frank Rogan, wearing a black, business suit. No Teflon. His beard hangs like overgrown weeds beneath his narrowed, reddened eyes.

"Stupid!" His breath exudes a sickly sweet smell. "You just don't know when to quit, do you?"

I shrug and avert my face. I'd do anything to avoid him if I could, right now.

"Even though you're half-dead, you managed to talk." Rogan leans over my bed, his face centimeters from mine. "That was a capital mistake."

So Kilroy listened to me after all.

"Richard Kilroy asked me what happened to Mary. I said I didn't know. Next thing, he holds a conference with Administration. In the meantime, the police turned up her body. They charged me with murder. Unfortunately for you, I got released on bail."

The chilling, reptilian directness of his gaze sends a shiver through me, clear to my bones. I feel like a mouse staring into the eyes of a hungry snake.

"I'm withdrawing the ventilator," Rogan's harsh whisper rasps near my ear. "Dead people can't talk, and besides, I've done everything I could to help you. So I'm letting you go."

"Frank, get away from her or I'll shoot." Kilroy emerges from the hallway with a weapon.

Rogan backs away a step, staring at Kilroy. "Put the gun down. Let's talk this over like professionals."

"Professionals? I suppose I could remind you of our first-do-no-harm rule, but I'd be wasting my breath. So let's focus on practicalities. Her people's technology runs centuries ahead of ours. If she dies, they might use it against us."

"Aw, come on, Kilroy!" Rogan frowns. "Her so-called people left her here."

"So they could dodge your bullets."The hostility in Kilroy's voice snaps in the quiet room. His weapon remains pointed at Rogan. "You've gotten careless and stupid."

"I think not." Rogan whips out his gun and I feel the cold barrel press against my head. "If you shoot, I'm taking her with me."

My ties and weakened condition prevent any attempt at physical escape. But I have the option of spirit travel, according to Mary.

"You wouldn't dare." Kilroy's voice is calm, but his face just paled.

"You've got a lovely wife and daughter." Rogan's lips tug up into a frosty smile. "Don't spoil it for yourself."

Kilroy's mouth opens and closes without a sound as he lowers his gun.

"That's better." Rogan's still smiling that cold, reptilian smile. "I suggest you leave. Quietly."

Kilroy edges toward the hall, his eyes wide and vulnerable. With both men's attention diverted, I disengage from my body and head for the computer.

"Keep moving," Rogan calls after his partner. "Keep--"

A bull roar emanates from inside the central processing unit. The virtual program opens with its garden scene, except now, harsh winds rattle the trees. The wind howls into the room, carrying with it the stink of decomposing flesh.

"What the...?" Rogan's mouth widens in terror and his gun drops. Something — a magnetic force like the kind generated by Athyr ships — pries his grip from my ventilator.

"Help!" The howling wind swallows Rogan's shout as his hands flail. The force pulls his thrashing form into the virtual garden.

Bony hands clutch Rogan's shoulders. The being I saw earlier — he looked like what humans call zombies — has hold of Rogan. Mouth opening wide to reveal rows of serrated teeth, it latches onto him, apparently determined to feed. Rogan's head goes in first, followed by his shoulders. Recoiling, I return to my body and concentrate on breathing with the ventilator. I turn my face toward the wall, trying hard to ignore the crunch of bones and the doctor's fading screams. Seconds pass like hours before the light fades and the virtual garden is gone.

The door opens, and a technician steps into my room. "What's going on? Kilroy ran out of here looking like he saw a ghost."

He pauses by the computer. Its screen glows neon blue, but the crunch continues, tinny and distant, somewhere in the central processing unit. The technician rolls his eyes. "Never mind."

****

It's been a week since Rogan disappeared. The breathing tube is finally out, and Kilroy's nurse replaced the ventilator with an oxygen mask. My throat burns, but my breath comes easy and my vital signs are steady.

"Doctor Kilroy mixed some new cream for your sores." After snapping on a light, the nurse removes my ties. She slathers my face and arms with green jelly. I tense, anticipating ungodly burning. Instead, the pain from my sores eases, replaced by blessed coolness. It will take a long time for me to relax and trust anyone around here, after Rogan.

The nurse retrieves an envelope from her pocket, tossing it onto my lap. "Someone left this for you."

I don't have to open it to know it contains the address for a certain ten-year-old boy with leukemia. After I recover, I have a promise to keep. A promise involving this child.

"Life," I whisper, and my lips curve into a smile.

The Good Samaritan

Panting for breath as she scrambled up the uneven slope, Laura Scott stumbled over battered skeletons. Oily, maroon liquid rippled through the bones, oozing into the sand beneath. Despite the cool air flowing through her pressurized blue suit, sweat trickled down her cheeks. A glance at her tanks warned she had ninety minutes of air before she asphyxiated. Maybe someday an explorer would stumble on her remains, too. Chills inched up her spine. Heart hammering in her chest, she gazed down the hill toward her spacecraft.

About six kilometers south, the tip of the bell-shaped Titan V peeped above a grove of skeletal leafless trees. The trees formed an ash-colored rib cage around the ship. Despite a fiery red sun overhead, the cement gray sky cast everything in shadow. Still, the sun hovered high above the ship and the trees, which arched toward her. Close as the shuttle appeared, the rocks and debris littering the slope made the distance too far to walk in ninety minutes. Laura rubbed her arms and shivered as she contemplated the events that led to her current predicament.

The Titan V left Earth three months ago, piloted by Captain O'Toole. He hoped to find a planet humans could colonize. Instead, his engine lost its hydraulic pressure, forcing an emergency landing on a glorified wasteland, with trees like petrified wood.

Laura suspected they contained lethal toxins, but she wasn't privy to the analyses of the soil and air done aboard ship, or their results. O'Toole's hostility toward Laura began and ended with scathing tirades. The impromptu landing hadn't improved his temper.

"You're a burden to my crew," he scolded her. "Kathy and the technicians are trying to fix our engine and figure out where we are. Maria is checking everyone for injuries. Thanks to the ridiculous community service requirement, we're saddled with a brain-damaged thief—a liar caught falsifying documents."

"I've worked in trauma care," she said in a trembling voice. "I can help Maria."

"Given your scrambled reflexes, I wouldn't let you treat my dog." Eyes glittering like tarnished silver, Captain O'Toole reached for his gun. He waved it toward a closet filled with pressurized suits. "Gear up. You're going for a walk."

With trembling fingers, Laura donned her suit and a backpack containing an air tank and other supplies.

"Keep moving." O'Toole spoke with a quiet intensity; the sound of metal tapping her glass helmet warned that he meant business. "In case you're thinking about coming back here another way...don't. You might have a nasty accident. Don't expect the others to come to your rescue."

The chills settled around Laura's neck. She looked at her tank. Eighty minutes of air left. The thick trees would provide hiding places for whatever killed the people whose bones she walked on. She felt through her backpack until her fingers closed around a ray gun. All the packs came equipped with weapons. The thing was, she hadn't used a gun since...When? She couldn't remember. What's more, O'Toole knew he could overpower her in a gunfight.

To hell with O'Toole. The others might want to know about my find.

Body trembling like a wire, Laura sprinted down the hill a few meters before pitching headlong in the dirt; her foot snagged on a felled tree. As she struggled to her knees, disbelief and fear pulsed through her.

A man wearing an ankle-length white tunic and black boots lay pinned beneath the tree, his mouth opening and closing like a guppy. Gently, she pried up an eyelid, revealing yellow eyes. His body was humanoid, but his features were extraterrestrial. His grunting breath whispered a rumor of broken ribs.

Laura gazed skyward, uncertain how to help him. Her laser gun could pulverize the tree but might set his clothes on fire. She had the training to assess his injuries and perform emergency procedures, but she knew nothing about his anatomy. Besides, skin contact could expose both of them to pathogens.

What difference will it make? If you do nothing, you'll both die.

Laura visualized the patients lining the cold tiled ward at the hospital where she once worked. They wept aloud, begging for medication, but they'd run short of money or insurance. Without funds, people couldn't get treatment. However, Laura knew her way around the computer labyrinth of loopholes and health insurance policies. By carefully doctoring charts, she saw to it her patients received treatment, regardless of their ability to pay. Some made a full recovery. In the end, her creative accounting cost her nursing license and her freedom.

She had no regrets—she'd do it again in a heartbeat. She reached for her gun. "Close your ears."

She knew he didn't understand her, but she felt better having said it.

The tree shivered and exploded under the gun's ray. Gray splinters and red dirt swirled through the air. The scattering chunks of petrified wood exposed the man's thin, quivering body. He continued gasping, his chest expansion uneven and ragged and his albino face the color of cement.

Laura retrieved her stethoscope from her backpack and examined him carefully. His hyper-resonant breath sounds on the right side and the way his trachea deviated to the left told her his shattered ribs had pierced his right lung. A needle decompression would relieve his symptoms, assuming his organs were similar to a human's, but the relief would be temporary. If he couldn't breathe, he'd die.

"This is going to hurt." She rooted through her emergency kit for a large-bore needle, disinfectant, and other necessary items for needle decompression.

She wedged the needle under his fourth rib and was rewarded with the hiss of escaping air. Within seconds, his breathing evened out. It wouldn't last. She needed to call for help.

Laura clicked on her wrist radio and hesitated. Who would help her? Not O'Toole. Nor would Kathy, since she answered to the captain. Taking a gamble, Laura paged Maria Ricci, a physician who seemed friendly. "Maria, this is Laura. Do you copy?"

Maria's buzzing voice indicated she heard.

"I found an extraterrestrial trapped under a tree on the hill about six kilometers north of the ship. He's unconscious but alive."

"An extraterrestrial? Really? Describe him."

"Except for his face, he looks human. He's wearing a white tunic and black boots. No air tank. He has broken ribs and a pneumothorax on his right side."

"That will require invasive… wait!" Maria's voice cracked with tension. "What have you done?"

Laura glanced at her tank, and sheer terror rolled through her, leaving a coppery taste in her mouth. "Needle decompression. I had no choice."

Laura heard a sigh over the radio. "I understand. O'Toole won't like risking contamination. I'll try to catch the shit when it hits the fan."

"You won't have to. I'll be dead before I get to the ship."

"*What?*"

"O'Toole held a gun to my back and ordered me to leave. He said I'd have a nasty accident if he saw me again. I have forty minutes left in my tank."

"He had no right to do that!"

"Someone forgot to tell him that."

Kathy's voice murmured in the background.

"Laura, set up some flares and sit tight," Maria's voice crackled over the connection. "Kathy and I are coming for you."

Moments later, a metallic blue rover cruised up the slope, with Kathy McDevitt—the orbital commander—at the wheel, and Maria beside her. Using the vehicle's mechanical arm, the three women lifted the injured man onto a stretcher.

"I never expected to meet a live alien," Kathy murmured, her green eyes widening. "According to my instruments, this planet is too hot and dry to support life."

Maria shifted her gaze between the trees and ship. "Maybe this fellow is a visitor. Captain O'Toole's going to freak out. Something's wrong with him."

"The engine's fixed." Kathy smiled. "That should put him in a good mood."

"Don't bet on it," Maria responded. "Laura, you and your friend are going to Isolation until we run blood cultures on both of you."

"Okay." Laura kept her gaze on her companion. The vehicle rattled and shook. His eyes opened and he winced. Moments later, the broad, circular hatchway on the side of the Titan V opened.

Kathy piloted the rover inside the lower deck. "Let's hurry before O'Toole sees us."

"I already saw you on the monitors," O'Toole's voice boomed from the control room. He raced down the steps, his nostrils flaring, face crimson, and his fists clenched. "Laura, what are you doing with that thing?"

Laura fidgeted, staring at the grid floor. "That *thing* is an injured man. He's got broken ribs and pneumothorax. I had to do needle decompression."

"Idiot! Didn't the possibility of contamination cross your pea-brain? Why didn't you report your findings straightaway?"

"Because you warned me not to..."

"You held a gun to her head, that's why," Maria cut in, anger flashing in her brown eyes. "You threatened her with 'a nasty accident'."

Laura watched the throbbing vein in O'Toole's neck, certain he'd pull out his weapon and shoot all of them any second now. His eyes narrowed and the muscles around on his face tightened.

"Oh, that."

"Yes, *that*." Maria crossed her arms over her chest. "She called me with her discovery. By the time Kathy and I brought them here, her tank was almost empty."

"Maria's right," Kathy put in. "If anything happens to Laura, the judge will order an investigation. You're right about contamination, though. We're moving them to Quarantine."

"Whatever." O'Toole shrugged. "Get them out of my sight."

Laura accompanied her patient into a sealed room with lead walls. Plastic gloves hung from portholes below its windows, enabling Maria to examine, x-ray, and treat the alien's injuries from outside the room. He squirmed as Maria's fingers made the incision to insert a chest tube. But the chest tube went in, and Maria taped up his chest as best she could. From previous experience, Laura knew that the lung would re-expand in a few days, but the ribs took weeks to heal.

After Maria finished with the alien, she employed a robotic mechanism to move his cot to the opposite side of the room. When she signaled for Heather to come to the window, Heather held out her arm for the blood draws she knew were forthcoming. Maria would want blood cultures, among other tests to rule out exposure to alien bacteria.

****

Hours after the tests were done, Laurel tiptoed toward his cot. "Maria didn't mean to hurt you. She was trying to help."

"I know." His silvery voice assured her. His hand lifted, grasping hers. His skin felt like cool silk.

Laura gasped. "You speak English?"

"My brain can process and translate vocal sounds, enabling me to assimilate your language. It takes several Earth-hours to do this." His yellow gaze never left her as he traced his finger along her hand. "Your anatomy is similar to ours. If your tank ran out, our atmosphere could have sustained you."

"Maybe." Laura managed a weak smile. "I'd need air-conditioning, though. Kathy says your temperature runs over fifty degrees Celsius."

"That's true." He smiled back. "I'm Pherseus. What should I call you?"

"My name is Laura."

"You knew how to help me without hesitance. Do you have medical training?"

"Yes and no. Before this flight, I treated sick people, as a nurse."

His yellow gaze never shifted. "How is it you found me?"

Laura averted her eyes, not caring to tell him what happened. Instead, she pretended he meant the crew as a whole. "Our ship developed engine trouble, and we made an emergency landing." She glanced out the window, but the hall appeared deserted. "Where are we?"

"Athyr. Very far from Earth. Your pilot must have crossed an invisible passage in space—a shortcut of sorts to an alternate galaxy. Any miscalculation can cause a crash landing."

"Our ship sustained damage, but no one got hurt." Laura rose and paced around the room. "Other travelers didn't get off so easy. I found human remains near where you had your accident."

"Those travelers may have been killed." Sorrow rolled through Pherseus' voice. "Fifteen years ago, a war broke out between the Crothians and my people. Before then, we lived above ground in a domed city called Helios. We traveled on streets lined with colorful shapes filled with helium, but the Crothians destroyed Helios. They seized control of Athyr, forcing us to migrate underground."

"That's awful. Will they attack this ship?"

"They might. During the day, they are dormant, but at night they search the land and disintegrate unwary visitors with their plasma guns. The untrained observer wouldn't even see them. Their armor camouflages them with the tree bark."

"If we use radar...hey!" Laura gasped as she looked down to see Pherseus standing, still with his chest tube, with one hand gripping the Pleura-vac container. "You shouldn't get out of bed without help."

Pherseus shrugged. "Why not? Our bodies are strong, and we heal fast. It takes much worse to confine someone like me to a bed. The pneumothorax and rib will take time to heal, but I will be all right. "

Laura's eyes widened. "I sure hope so. Many humans hibernate in bed until the doctors are ready to remove the chest tube—usually days, and it can take weeks for broken ribs to heal. Sometimes we have complications, such as infection of the wound or pneumonia."

"What is pneumonia?"

"The lungs fill with fluid, especially in frail, elderly people. Bacteria or viruses can cause this. We use drugs to treat pneumonia." Laura gulped, fighting an onslaught of tears. "Assuming the patient can pay for them."

"What do you mean by 'patient'?"

"At home, we called the sick and injured under our care 'patients.' The protocol is different here because we've never met people from other worlds. Kathy and Maria were intrigued about working with you."

"I can appreciate that." Pherseus nodded, then peered through the windows. "I'd like to see more of your ship. Will these women keep us here a long time?"

"Until they get the results of their blood tests, yes." Laura bit her lip. "We could have infected each other since I did an invasive procedure. It takes about two days for most bacteria to show."

"I understand. Maria — your healer — seemed worried. Your captain is furious. I am sorry I caused everyone trouble."

The ward patients came to mind again, their desperate cries echoing from the tiled hall. Laura imagined their contorted bodies writhing against the restraints. She could still smell the pus oozing from their untreated bed sores.

Tears slid down her face.

Pherseus' cool hand rested on her shoulder, nudging her back to the present. "My people can read minds. Right now, you're reliving a nightmare involving the sick."

Laura shook her head. "It's nothing."

Pherseus' eyes widened. "How can you say it's nothing? You are frightened and upset."

Laurel heaved a sigh. It wasn't like he could do anything with the information. More to the point, his gentle voice invited trust.

"It happened back home. I chose to help sick people with treatable illnesses. I fixed their documents so their insurance companies — third-party payers — would pay for their care." She blotted more tears from her eyes. "My patients got better, but my actions cost me my license."

"What license? I do not understand."

"Where I come from, we can't practice medicine without written permission from our government. If a patient's insurance coverage expires, we're supposed to stop treatment, whether the condition is curable or not. This includes routine therapies, comfort drugs, and life support. My actions saved lives, but I committed insurance fraud."

"Why did you choose that work, knowing the barriers?" Pherseus' tone implied curiosity without judgment or shock.

"Up until five years ago, I was a pilot for United Aeronautics. I don't recall the details, but an explosion left me with head injuries and amnesia. The injury affected my reflexes, so the doctors told me I couldn't fly anymore." Laura looked away. "Hospitals will hire people with medical histories like mine because they're desperate for workers."

"My father said severe trauma causes amnesia in humans," Pherseus told her. "What happened after your superiors caught you altering their documents?"

"The hospital administrators had me arrested, and there was a trial. After reviewing my work record, the judge sentenced me to community service — this space flight. I thought I was getting off easy until I met Captain O'Toole." She lowered her voice to a whisper. "He held a gun to my back and ordered me to leave the ship and not come back. I assume you understood the conversation between him and Maria."

Pherseus nodded, rubbing his chin. "Your captain seems like a dangerous man. How will he treat someone like me?"

"That's a good question." Laura shivered, uneasy. "According to my file, O'Toole and I worked together before the explosion, and he acts like he remembers me. I don't remember meeting him before this flight."

"Maybe I help you." Pherseus sat up. "My society's technology can unlock the subconscious."

"Technology?" Laura arched her eyebrows. "I went to a world-renowned neurologist and psychiatrist, and neither could help me remember."

"My doctors could help you," Pherseus pressed. "Because the war left so many casualties, they learned how to treat traumatic brain injuries."

"I see." Laura nodded in agreement. "You've got technology we don't have. You had to find ways to survive and treat those casualties."

"That is right. Our equipment can analyze and reproduce any living tissue, including that of humans. Our doctors could augment your brain function with cell cloning and neurostimulation."

Laura's fingers trembled as she brushed wisps of blonde hair from her forehead. "Cloning? Neurostimulation? Our doctors have done neurostimulation in certain diseases, but that wasn't an option for me."

"It is now. My father is a general and has traveled to your world to study humans. He wore a disguise, and since most humans don't acknowledge the existence of life on foreign worlds, no one questioned the disguise."

Laura shifted uncomfortably. "That's because our neighboring planets have hostile environments. How will you do such procedures? Will your doctors even treat humans?"

"They will if my father gives the orders. While you were resting, I regained full consciousness and spoke with my father. He expressed his willingness to help you because you saved my life. Our doctors use tiny probes to stimulate the neurons and inject the cloned cells. These will augment your reflexes."

"Augment?" Hope crept into Laura's voice. "Would this enable me to fly again?"

"It might. I'd like to take you to meet my family tomorrow night while your shipmates are asleep. By then, Maria should have her blood test results, and I should be recovered enough to travel."

Laura hesitated, fingering the hairline scars in her scalp. "I'd settle for recalling my life before the explosion. I appreciate the offer, but it sounds risky. Most procedures involving the brain are."

"So is working for your captain. If you survive this flight, what kind of work will you do after you fulfill your community requirement?"

"I don't know." Laura drew in a sharp breath. She hadn't thought that far ahead. Up until a few hours ago, she was facing death. "Nursing's no longer an option."

"The treatment can make those other positions attainable, and you will be able to protect yourself from your captain and the Crothians." Pherseus took her hands in his, his voice kind. "You saved my life when you pulled me from under that tree. Let me save yours."

Laura gazed toward the door, with its electronic locks. "The door to this quarantine room and the hatchway are locked. The airlock maintains a stable temperature and oxygen environment here. Those locks wouldn't stop you from getting us out of here, right?"

"I can deactivate the electronic fields on all your locks, yes."

"How will we get to your underground city? We have a vehicle, but only Kathy and Captain O'Toole know how to use it. And with that chest tube, it will be hard for you to walk."

"Who said we were going to walk? My father's sending over his vehicle. He located your ship on his viewscreen. Once we get to my home, a healer there will remove the chest tube, seal the puncture, and the rib will heal with time."

Laura thought again about O'Toole's cold eyes and malignant grin as he brandished his gun. The fate of unemployed people with medical problems flashed through her mind, next. She fingered the plastic card in her pocket—her now-defunct nursing license. "All right. Let's do it."

****

Because Athyr had no moon, a jet black sky shrouded the landscape when Laura and Pherseus left the shuttle. The blue headlights of the teardrop-shaped vehicle—piloted by an android—cut swords across the dry, cracked soil. A side door slid open. Pherseus ushered her onboard into a cushioned rear seat, then sat beside her. "We'll stay away from the trees. This will help us to avoid the Crothians," Pherseus said. "Sitting in the back will keep us out of their direct range of fire, too."

Laurel shuddered. She'd forgotten about the Crothians. "They won't bother us since they've got their territory." She gazed at Pherseus, pleading for reassurance. "Right?"

"We never signed any treaty. We avoid trouble by staying out of their way. If a Crothian approaches, shoot it. Your plasma gun should work."

Panic seared through Laura, turning her skin to gooseflesh. "I can't shoot anyone. The thought of handling guns makes me sick."

"Make an exception. If the Crothian shoots first, his laser will burn you to ashes."

"Oh, no," Laura groaned. "I wish you'd told Maria or Kathy. They would have listened."

"They might, but they answer to your Captain O'Toole."

"True." Laura gripped the armrests as the android steered hard to avoid fallen branches. "Have you ever killed a Crothian?"

"More than once. The first time, my parents and I were living in Helios. Then the Crothians elected Theseus as their governor. He promised peace, but his officials made slaves of my people. They punished most crimes by death."

"Why?"

"Theseus lusted after power. His army guarded the cities by shooting would-be escapees or visitors on sight. If a slave displeased them, the soldiers tortured them and hosted summary executions."

"That's terrible!" Laura tensed as something dark—an animal, perhaps—scuttled through the sandy soil to their left. Shining her flashlight, she made out two drifting branches. With a deep sigh, she turned her attention back to Pherseus. "How did you escape?"

"My father developed a neurostimulator like the one you will receive tonight. He organized an army and instructed his surgeon to perform the procedure on his soldiers. Their reflexes improved, and they were able to fight the Crothians and build tunnels to underground cities."

"Your father's a survivor." Laura fought to control the tremor in her voice. "Was Theseus or any of the other Crothians able to mind-read your father's plans?"

"The Crothians can read minds, but unlike them, we can communicate telepathically from far away. Thankfully, my father had no personal contact with Theseus, so this gave him an advantage" Pherseus heaved a sigh. "Thousands of people joined my father. Half of them died, including my mother. When my father arrived at the underground city, he realized my mother was missing. He sent out a search team, and days after that, they found her body in the ruins."

"I'm sorry." Compassion and sorrow tugged at Laura. "That must have been awful for you!"

"It was. If these people attack your shuttle, I cannot help you." Despair edged into his voice. "We cannot bomb their camps without wrecking an underground city. Their armor enables them to blend in with the trees. Can anyone make your captain understand this?"

"O'Toole won't appreciate any warnings from me, but he listens to his crew, and I think at least some of them will listen to me." Laura turned up the lights attached to her helmet, trying to get a better look at her surroundings, but she saw nothing but sand and darkness. "How much further do we have to go?"

"A kilometer ahead, we shall stop at a rock cave."

The android parked in the cave. Pherseus motioned her out of the vehicle and climbed out after her. After he walked her into the cave, pink lights circled them. Moments later, she found herself in a dimly lit tiled corridor. Two women wearing white-helmeted suits emerged from a doorway. Pherseus conversed quietly with them for a moment, then turned back toward Laura. "My father needs time to assimilate your language, and I need to be seen by another healer. We shall talk after you get your implants."

Laura nodded, mesmerized by her surroundings. She followed the women to a chamber with terracotta slate walls and marble pillars. Computers and other machinery circled a sheet-covered table. The women removed Laura's suit, slipped a white robe over her shoulders, and led her to the table. Despite the solid metal against her back, her eyes felt heavy, and her lids closed. Pinpricks raced along her scalp. The machinery whispered soft, shushing noises inside her ears, lulling her to sleep.

The shushing gave way to a man's panicked voice.

****

"Captain!" The voice sounded familiar, but Laura couldn't place it. "Captain Scott, we have an emergency. Someone broke into the warehouse."

Laura turned her head, surprised to find herself in an office at United Aeronautics. She blinked as recognition dawned. This was *her* office, before the explosion.

Responding to the call for help, she grabbed a flashlight and crept down a gloomy hall. No sign of intruders. At the warehouse, her light washed over aisles of air pumps and other equipment. She closed her free hand over her weapon as she called out, "Hello? Is anyone here?"

No answer, except the humming compressors.

As she cleared the rear corner, something hard slammed her in the back, and she stumbled and fell. Looking up, she found a man dressed in white pointing a gun at her. She scrambled to bring her weapon up, but before she could, he fired. Searing agony exploded through her head.

****

Stabbing pain jarred Laura awake. Memories of United Aeronautics faded, replaced by unfamiliar surroundings. As her vision cleared, she saw Pherseus minus his chest tube and another man beside the table. Fine lines creased the stranger's face, dimpling at his pointed chin.

"Laura, this is my father, Ares." Pherseus indicated the stranger. "He authorized your treatment."

"I was glad to help." Admiration brightened Ares expression. "It was the least I could do after you rescued my son."

"Thank you." Laura raised quaking fingers to her head, to encounter thick bandages. The echo of remembered gunfire thrummed through her mind, and she swore she still smelled the sulfur baking off the gun barrel from the warehouse. "I've got an awful headache."

"Brain surgery leaves most people with headaches." Ares handed Laura a glass of green liquid. "Drink this. You will feel better."

Laura drained the contents of the glass. Not bad. It tasted like lime juice, and her headache was already subsiding.

"Pherseus said an accident left you with questions about your past" Ares studied her with open concern. "I hope the answers bring you peace."

"I hope so, too." Bits of memories flashed through her consciousness like glass shards. She grimaced. "Pherseus told me about your war with the Crothians."

Ares' expression hardened. "Pherseus understated the danger. These people wreck cities to acquire slaves. Their radar can sense movement kilometers away."

"My captain parked his shuttle above ground near the sandy area."

"He used bad judgment. The Crothians prowl the sands at night, and they will attack his vehicle."

"I've got to warn them. By now, Maria must realize I'm missing. What if she looks for me while it's dark? Where's my pressure suit?"

She sat up and threw her legs over the table. Waves of dizziness assaulted her, and she swayed. Pherseus and Ares caught her by the shoulders and eased her back onto the table.

"Your concern is admirable," Ares soothed, "but you are in no condition to travel. Pherseus, find her people and warn them about the Crothians."

"Consider it done." Pherseus headed for the door.

Watching him go, Laura closed her eyes and voiced a silent prayer that he and all her shipmates would be safe.

****

"Captain Scott!" The anxious voice was back, and United Aeronautics materialized around her, once again.

This was a dream. It had to be a dream, she realized hazily, as the exact sequence of events replayed, right up to the gun firing and searing agony burning through her head.

Laura's eyes snapped open to the terracotta slate walls of her cubicle. Pherseus stood by her table, with a lanky woman with shoulder-length wavy hair and olive complexion beside him. "Maria wanted to see you."

Maria clutched her helmet against her chest. Her swollen, reddened eyes told Laura she'd been crying. "What have these people done to you? You look awful."

"I'm all right." Laura attempted a smile. Her lips couldn't complete the motion just yet. "I don't see pink elephants or anything."

"It's not funny." Maria stared at Laura, eyes huge, while wiping her eyes. "How could you let these people drive nails into your brain?"

"I'm hoping this surgery will enable me to fly again, or at least recall what happened before the explosion. It was their way of thanking me for helping Pherseus." Laura averted her gaze. She didn't want to mention her dream about the warehouse just yet. "We've got trouble, Maria. Did Pherseus tell you about the Crothians?"

Maria nodded. "Kathy collected tissue samples from the remains when we found you the other day. She gave O'Toole the results. He seemed interested."

Laura sat up, rubbing her eyes. "I imagine he'd be concerned."

"He doesn't give a damn about anyone's welfare." Maria drew in a deep breath. "He tried to detain your friend for questioning. His worries about contamination ended when he considered the potential financial rewards. Kathy distracted him so Pherseus and I could leave."

"Kathy's piloting skills give her leverage. "A dry laugh pushed from Laura. "We owe her one."

Footsteps clicked from the hall. Pherseus' father emerged through the doorway. "Are you feeling better?" he asked.

"A little."

"Unlike the techniques used by humans, our surgeries are minimally invasive, and recovery is quick," Ares told her. "Nevertheless, you should stay here until you heal and we evaluate the effectiveness of the treatment. The Crothians will not bother you here. You are welcome to stay, too, Maria. Pherseus speaks well of you."

Pain knifed through Laura's head. Looking up, she saw fear written in Maria's almond eyes.

How could Laura trust total strangers? Her thought read like a printed text.

Laura shifted her eyes toward Pherseus whose eyes were wide with concern.

I made trouble for Laura. His thoughts were clear, too.

"What's wrong, Laura?" Ares was watching her with concern.

"I'm not sure." Laura touched her head but only felt the bandages. "Pherseus, you didn't cause any trouble, and Maria, I, ah..." She looked toward Ares again. "Why am I reading everyone's thoughts?"

"The implants will stimulate the dormant parts of your brain. When they reach the full effect, you will be able to reach minds miles away."

"What about my memory?"

"Listen to your dreams. Your memory will return when you are ready to accept the past."

Laura gazed at her visitors, debating whether or not to discuss her dream. She recalled creeping through the warehouse, and the gunfire. She dared not mention United Aeronautics — not with her attacker's face now clear in her memory.

O'Toole shot her.

"Laura told me she used to fly before her accident," Pherseus was explaining to his father when she surfaced from her thoughts. "I'd like to show her our space vehicles. I'd also like to show her and Maria how to handle our plasma weapons, in case the Crothians invade their ship."

"Not only the Crothians," Maria agreed. "O'Toole is up to something ugly."

"Then we shall train you." Ares' voice rang with finality.

Laura wrapped the sheet around her shoulders, shivering. She gazed toward the door.

"Laura, what's wrong?" Maria's voice was gentle as she touched a hand to Laura's shoulder.

"I can't handle any firearm." Laura swallowed hard, her teeth chattering. "I...Oh, forget it."

"Your eyes speak volumes." Ares' gaze met and locked with hers. He was reading her memory of the warehouse, but she sensed understanding mixed with infinite sadness. "Getting shot is not an easy pain. Your injuries may heal, but the fear makes a home in your heart. Sometimes it whispers and you hardly know it is there. Other times, it hits you like a deadly ray, and everything inside screams at you to run."

He paused. Then, "You've got to ignore your pain."

"I don't think I can." Laura hated the waver in her voice.

"My reading taught me forcing humans into battle can have devastating effects." Ares regarded Laura as a scientist studying a prized specimen. "Laura, you risked prison to get medicines needed for people under your care. Despite your proximity to death, you extricated my son from under a tree and treated his injuries. Now you are worried about your shipmates. How will you forgive yourself if someone dies because you were too afraid to fight?"

"This is..." *different,* Laura was about to say, but it wasn't. She thought about the patients she saved by retooling their insurances, then Pherseus, trapped under the tree and pleading for help. Suppose he or one of her patients died because she was afraid? *Diggity damn, Ares struck the nail on the head. No wonder he's such a successful leader.*

"I couldn't." Laura met her companions' gazes. "I'll give it my best try."

Though she saw the questions in her friend's eyes, Maria never asked why guns frightened her, so Laura didn't volunteer information. She imagined, sooner or later, Maria would ask. Laura just wasn't sure how to answer.

****

As it turned out, treatments, target practice, and underground tours left no time for confidences. As Ares promised, Laura healed fast, and after two weeks, her headaches subsided completely. Memories or not, with the headaches finally gone, it was time she faced O'Toole and the Crothians. Pherseus walked Laura and Maria to their rover.

"I hate saying goodbye." Laura frowned at Pherseus. "I feel as if I'm losing a good friend."

"But you must leave, now, if you are to save your shipmates. The Crothians will attack."

"I know." Despite her padded suit, Laura managed a small hug. "Thank you for helping me to find the truth."

"Be careful." Pherseus waved his hands. Pink rays engulfed Laura and Maria, beaming them above ground.

When she and Maria finally arrived back at the Titan, Kathy was pacing around the dining area.

"Where have you guys been?" She rounded on them immediately. "O'Toole's given me nothing but grief since you disappeared with our visitor. He's had me comb this wasteland looking for you."

Maria shrugged. "He's more upset about his rover than he is about Laura and me."

Before Kathy could reply, feet clattered on the stairs. The color drained from her face, making her freckles stand out like raised dots. She bolted to the lower deck.

"How dare you disobey me?" O'Toole ticked off their transgressions on his thick fingers, "Using the rover without authorization, failing to notify me of your whereabouts, losing my prized specimen..."

"Pherseus is a person, not a 'specimen'."

"Whatever. It was valuable to me."

"Well, *he* is gone," Laura shot back. "We tried to tell you where we were, but we got static on the radio."

"Liar!" O'Toole slammed his fist against the wall. "All the rovers have new radios. Where did you hide?"

"Why do you care?" Laura challenged him. "You told me not to come back here."

O'Toole was in her face faster than she could blink.

"Idiot," he whispered, and Laura gagged on the cloying odor of his cologne. "Who gave you food and water?"

"I did," Maria replied, glowering at O'Toole. "Laura and her companion were not safe here, because of you. Regardless of what you think of her, *I* saw something in Laura worth saving. I did what I needed to protect her from you."

"So both of you helped it get away." O'Toole backed away, crooking his finger. "Follow me."

At the lower deck, he led them past Isolation to a steel gray door marked *Experiments*. O'Toole typed on a keypad panel by the door. "This room simulates different levels of gravity. It makes a great disciplinary tool. Inside. Both of you."

"Forget it." Laura shook her head. "I'm not going into any room you tell me. Not after you tried to have me killed." Laura cut her gaze toward Maria. "What say you?"

"Hell, no!" Maria folded her arms across her chest. "We did nothing wrong."

"Careful! My camera records all the interaction that takes place on this ship." O'Toole tapped the beige disk on his pressurized suit. "The laws for the military apply to this mission. Disobeying an officer can land you in jail."

"The hell you say!" Maria glared at him. "That rule only applies to lawful orders. What you're asking is illegal."

"The courts might not think so. Because you two are in this together, a court-martial might also construe your behavior as attempted mutiny, in which case both of you would be sentenced to death. Especially since ..." O'Toole gave Laura a crooked, rather malignant grin. "...you've already got a record."

Maria heaved a sigh, then shot Laurel a questioning look.

"We'd better do as he says," Laurel said in a dismal voice. "The ship's also got flight recorders that track everything — one of the things I remember from my past."

The door slid open like a gaping toothless mouth. Laura shuffled inside, followed by Maria. The door closed behind them, and Laura's body became a lead weight. She sagged against the wall. "I feel like I gained 100 pounds. What happened?"

"He set the gravity way high, that's what." Maria glared at the airlock. "You won't get away with this, Captain."

"I already have." O'Toole's laughter crackled over the intercom. "You'll do calisthenics until I say stop. I'll watch from the monitors upstairs. Now, move it."

Sweat bathed Laura's body as she attempted sit-ups. Her arms and shoulders drooped like cooked spaghetti. "You shouldn't have lied for me, Maria. Now he has it in for you, too."

"I wouldn't have it any other way." Maria panted between each word. "What you did at the hospital took guts. I'm sorry you got caught."

"So am I, Maria." Laura flopped on the floor, gasping for air, when she sensed O'Toole wasn't watching. "So am I."

After what felt like hours, but was probably just minutes, beeping sounded from the hallway, and the door slid open to reveal a tearful but resolute Kathy. She wasn't the cheerful pilot Laura knew, anymore. She wore the expression of a battle-weary soldier -- someone on the receiving end of one too many denigrations by a tyrannical superior.

"I was supposed to watch you guys while O'Toole looks for Pherseus." Kathy's voice was bitter. "That's bull. You can rest now."

"Thanks." Maria sank to the floor in relief. "I need a shower."

"Me, too." Laura struggled to her feet. "Kathy, what happened?"

"O'Toole's been making everyone miserable since he took over at Aeronautics. Now he's out of control." Kathy regarded them with shadowed eyes. "Where were you two?"

"Pherseus showed us his underground city." Laura sighed in relief as the gravity evened out. "We saw his vehicles, and I reminisced about my flying days. Did you know I used to captain this shuttle?"

Kathy wiped her eyes and smoothed back her auburn hair. "No, I didn't."

"Would you mind if I had a look at the flight controls? Also, I'd like to know what calculations you made to get here."

Kathy arched her rust-colored brows. "I used warp drive, but the calculations are complicated. Why do you want to know?"

"Pherseus' doctors injected cloned brain cells and neurostimulators to build up my reflexes," Laura told her. "Now I remember everything I did before the explosion, including flying the Titan V. I want to see how well I remember the fine details."

"O'Toole will lose it if he sees you."

"Don't worry about O'Toole. I can tell where he's going and what he's about to do. He'll never catch me."

Kathy's eyes widened with fear. "How can you say that?"

"The Athyrians—the people who treated me—can read minds. Their implants stimulated dormant areas of my brain, so now I can read people's minds."

Kathy gaped at her. "Are you serious?"

"I'm one hundred percent serious." Laurel smiled at Kathy. "For example, before you came down here, you were playing some computer game."

"Busted!" Kathy broke into laughter. "It sounds like you fell down a well of shit and came up with diamonds. All right, Laura, let's go to the cockpit. I went to hear everything about your adventures."

****

Laura and Maria joined the rest of the crew for a dinner of canned chili and beans that evening. The crew studiously avoided looking at them, and the tinkle of silverware punctuated the silence.

"What's wrong with everyone?" Maria wanted to know.

Laura glanced toward O'Toole.

"Later," she whispered.

O'Toole looked up, glaring at them. "Stop whispering. If you have something to say, say it."

"How did your search go?" Laura inquired.

"I didn't find my specimen." O'Toole gave her a censuring glare. "We're not leaving until we capture an Athyrian or Crothian."

"How do you propose we do that?" Maria shot back. "From what Pherseus says, the Crothians are vicious."

"We keep our eyes on the viewscreens for trouble." O'Toole's smile didn't reach his glittering eyes. "Since you and Laura are good buddies, you two watch the viewscreens. Starting tonight."

With an evil smirk, he dumped his garbage and strolled out of the room.

"It gets worse by the second." Maria shook her head. "Get some sleep, Laura. You'll need it."

Darkness draped the world outside when Laura and Maria settled at the viewscreens. The ship's lights cast bright circles on a blue-suited figure digging through the soil. Laura sat up and started.

"I don't believe this! Kathy's collecting soil samples."

"Now?" Maria rolled her eyes. "Is she trying to get herself killed?"

"I don't think so." Laura focused on Kathy, trying to reach into her mind. "I talked to her about flying and how I remember things before the explosion. I sensed O'Toole terrorized her. She blames herself for the explosion, even though O'Toole was the one who shot me." Laura reached for her plasma weapon. "Sit tight. I'll talk to her."

Laura scooted down the steps. She paced ten meters from the ship. Ten more. "Kathy," she called, shining her flashlight. "Kathy!"

No answer.

"Kathy," Laura called, her voice urgent. Seconds later, she found Kathy knee-deep in brown grass twenty-five meters from the ship.

"What's the matter?" she asked, shaking Kathy's shoulder. "Why didn't you answer me?"

"My phones were turned off." Kathy rose to her feet. "I came out here to think. There's no reason we can't leave. If O'Toole keeps going after those Crothians, he'll get us killed."

"We can talk, but not here. Let's go..." Plodding footsteps echoed from the north, impinging on Laura's thoughts. She shuddered. "Too late. We have a visitor."

Kathy craned her neck. "I don't see anyone."

"I don't either, but the footsteps sound like some-one or something heavy. It's coming from those trees to our left. Turn up your phones and listen hard. Hear it?"

Kathy nodded. "Let's head back to the ship."

Keeping close to Kathy, Laura started toward the ship while darting a glance toward the trees. Their gnarled trunks blended, giving off a uniform gray look.

Seconds later, a shape emerged from behind the trees. The ship's lights illuminated a figure wearing what looked like sheaves of tree bark. The figure's gloved hand brandished a gun.

"It's coming after us," Kathy whispered. "I'll stay out here. You run to the ship and get help."

Eyes glued to the ship, Laura saw the Crothian about thirty meters from where they knelt. "Whoever goes after it will be fried. You run, and I'll stay. The others need you alive to get them home."

"You know how to fly this shuttle, too." Kathy shook her head. "Besides, you've gotten punished for trying to save lives. I committed a real crime and have yet to pay my dues. I saw O'Toole shoot the former administrator."

Laura gasped. *"What?"*

"I was doing inventory when I overheard O'Toole's boss reprimand him, and not for the first time either. Sometime later, I heard gunfire from the warehouse. O'Toole shot his boss in the head. I called an ambulance and told them there'd been an explosion."

"An explosion?" Laura grimaced, her throat dry as sandpaper. "I was his boss, Kathy. I'd gotten another complaint about O'Toole's temper. He came across calm and willing to listen, but right before the so-called explosion, he lured me to the warehouse, saying we had intruders."

Kathy's face turned pale as paper. "You remember all that?"

"Yes, and more. Why didn't you tell the police?"

"O'Toole threatened to kill me. He reinforced his warning by shooting my brother." Straightening, Kathy edged toward the clearing. "I wrecked your life. This is my chance to balance the scales. Let me do this, Laura."

"All right."

Laura edged out behind Kathy. She watched while Kathy fired at the Crothian and struck true. After that, she broke into her run for the Titan. Her shoes thudded against the grass, dull thumps that became squishy and liquid. Looking down, she saw the reason why: fire from Kathy's gun had only crumbled the figure's left arm, and now, dark slime was flowing down the slope. A scream came and died in her throat.

Red lasers flared toward Kathy, igniting her suit into flames. She let out horrible, choked howls, audible despite her visor. Something inside Laura died at the sound of them. She turned, bracing for another sprint toward the ship, then froze. The figure was coming toward her.

Her hand shook as she aimed her gun at the Crothian. She saw herself at the warehouse again, facing O'Toole. The blast shuddered through her memory, followed by the horrible smell of sulfur. The Crothian was twenty meters away and closing.

This isn't the warehouse. Shoot it!

Her blast scattered chunks of armor. Orange sparks shot skyward. Screaming, Laura bolted through the airlock and turned toward the flight deck.

"Maria, hurry! Kathy's hurt."

Maria glanced toward the viewscreen by the door, showing Kathy's charred body and clothing tatters. A bloody maw stretched from ear to ear, with pink and gray matter dribbling from one side. "There's no point in hurrying, Laura. Kathy's gone."

"She can't be gone. If we work together, we can save her."

"Laura, her head injuries are too severe. Before your implant, that Crothian would've gotten you, too. You did great, Laura."

"I don't feel so great." Standing beside Maria, Laura stared at the monitor. "Kathy told me the truth about my head injury, but I remember everything. That night, O'Toole asked me to investigate some noises, and instead..." Hot, salty tears stung her eyes. "I should have known he was setting me up. Why did I let him trick me?"

"Because you're a kind person who sees the good in people. That's why you trusted Pherseus so readily. You didn't deserve to be shot."

"Kathy said he shot her brother," Laura confided, sorrow gripping her. "It was his way of warning her to keep quiet."

"Now he's running this ship." Maria's frightened gaze shifted toward the door. "With Kathy gone, we're on our own."

Clicking footsteps echoed from the hall. O'Toole's.

"Pull yourself together before he sees you." Maria prodded Laura toward the lavatory.

Laura washed and dried her face. When she returned, O'Toole stood at the door, eyeballing the monitors.

"I can't believe this happened to Kathy," he shouted. "What was she doing outside?"

"Beats me," Maria replied in a dull voice. "Laura shot the Crothian. You'll see its remains on monitor C."

O'Toole looked up and started, his silver eyes wide as saucers. The viewscreen showed tendrils of smoke billowing from skeletal remains, melted plates, and a pool of red filmy liquid. "Laura, did you really do that?"

Laura shrugged. "You can watch the video. Kathy and I were outside when the thing approached." She pointed to screen A. "You can see the damage its lasers can do."

O'Toole watched the video and nodded. "Let's haul that specimen aboard. Put on a shield and load its remains into a lead container. This find will earn millions."

Maria glared at him. "Is that wise? Its remains might secrete toxins."

"I don't care." O'Toole's expression turned thunderous. "I'm Captain. I give the orders."

"Oh, yeah?" Maria went toe-to-toe with him, her glare cutting. "I'm the ship's physician, and you won't have a job if I report you."

Out of the corner of her eye, Laura saw O'Toole go for his gun, his eyes full of the same murderous intent as when he cornered her in the warehouse. She hated that look, but she knew what it meant. O'Toole was preparing to shoot Maria and her.

"Captain, you're right." She stepped forward, playing along. "We have a gold mine."

"You got that right."

"Why would you trust idiots like us with this sensitive material? If you pack the remains, Maria and I will carry them to the ship."

O'Toole squinted, and she could hear his thoughts turning over her words. A slow, crafty grin spread across his face. "I couldn't have said it better, Laura. Meet me outside as soon as possible."

He strode away, whistling to himself.

"What are you doing?" Maria demanded once he was gone. "Why are you agreeing with that creep?"

"Who said I was? He was about to shoot both of us. I was playing along with him, that's all. If more Crothians show, we can run and let O'Toole take the heat."

"I'm sorry." Maria sighed. "I keep forgetting you can read minds. We'd better change. He'll be expecting us."

****

After suiting up and stowing plasma guns into their tool belts, Laura and Maria joined O'Toole outside the ship. Already, he was shoveling melted plates and debris into a box, pausing only for a cursory nod. Distant, rumbling footsteps echoed through the landscape, but so far, no other sign of movement. Smoke wafted from the creature's remains. Intent on his task, O'Toole gave no sign of hearing the heavy footsteps. Moments later, the trees to their left shifted.

Not the trees. Crothians. Laura shivered at the horrible realization.

"They're coming!" She nudged Maria, and they sprinted to the ship.

Halfway to safety, Laura darted a glance over her shoulder. Three Crothians were coming around O'Toole on the rubble. Lasers flared. His screams drowned out the sound of the crackling flames, truncated as the Crothians fell upon him.

"Laura, duck!" Maria shouted.

Laura scooted sideways, dodging a laser by centimeters. She then turned and fired at her pursuer. An ear-splitting blast filled the air, followed by two more.

"I got the other two!" Maria yelled. "More are coming from the mountains. Let's go!"

"I hope someone can fly the shuttle," Laura said.

You know how to fly this shuttle, too, Kathy's voice echoed in her mind.

"That was five years ago," she whispered to herself. With Maria at her heels, she hurried to the flight deck, where three technicians were monitoring the screens.

"Everyone, listen up," Maria called. "We must leave this planet. Can anyone fly this shuttle?"

The technicians exchanged looks and began murmuring among themselves.

"Then we're headed for trouble." Alarm colored Maria's voice. "The Crothians are coming for our ship."

Laura glanced at the viewscreen. Six more Crothians plodded toward the ship. She had no time to think.

"I've flown this thing more than once." Grim confidence filled her as she plopped into the cockpit. "Everyone belt in. I am going to have to make this shuttle do some tricks."

"What tricks?" A technician's nervous voice echoed in the flight deck. "You're not supposed to be flying."

Maria laughed with relief. "If Laura says she can get us out of here, she will."

Laura glanced at the close-up view of the approaching Crothians on her screen. Her fingers ran over the buttons, initiating the launch sequence. Smoke flared outside the portholes, before she was thrown against her seat and the shuttle roared into the atmosphere.

About 48 hours later, her stomach dropped as if the Titan V had taken a nosedive. She squeezed her eyes shut and gripped her armrests. Colors floated in grotesque shapes under her eyelids.

The ship's speed leveled off. Laura opened her eyes. When she glanced at the instrument panels, they were heading into warp drive. She smiled.

Turning around, she saw a technician clutching his stomach.

"Are we going to have this crap for the rest of the flight?" he muttered.

"I hope not. It's a three-month flight." Laura laughed as his face turned a sick shade of green. "You'd better take something for your motion sickness."

"You handled that beautifully," Maria praised her. "Maybe United Aeronautics will give you back your old job. You think?"

Laura hesitated as she read the technicians' anxious thoughts. She shifted her gaze toward the beige disk on her suit, the one that tracked her movements and voice, then to the one on Maria's suit. Her gaze then moved around the flight area where the flight recorders were kept. No doubt everything that happened—O'Toole forcing her off the ship, her meeting with Pherseus and stay at his compound, and the shootout with the Crothians—would become public record. She and Maria could expect to face questioning by the authorities.

But there was also this. She had no regrets, and if she went to jail, she would do so with her head held high. In any case, she had a three-month flight, and so maybe her worries could be postponed for another day. She looked back at Maria and fetched a deep sigh.

"That, my friend, is a good question. Right now, I just want to get us home."

The Forgotten Ward

Only moments before she went into cardiac arrest, Anne input medication orders to a computer for transmission to a humanoid robot. Aware it went against hospital rules, she programmed the robot to deliver medicines to the Forgotten Ward during shift report. The ward held thirty patients whose treatments were on hold until they or their families could pay for their care. Change-of-shift report lasted a half hour, but the 2050 robots made every second count. If Administration discovered what she did, they would send Anne to jail. Anne ensured her anonymity by using homemade software capable of hiding her tracks. Still, the best-laid schemes could fail.

"Anne!" Anne jerked upright at the sharp crack of her boss' voice.

"I saw you and John whispering to each other during report this morning." Anne's boss, Lorraine Bogle, leaned against the door frame, gray-suited arms folded against her chest. Her blue eyes glittered like ice chips. The dour-faced portraits lining the hall outside held more warmth than Lorraine's chiseled features. "What was so fascinating?"

"We were discussing a patient case." The lie and smile came easily, even as pressure built below her sternum. Without her medicine, sharp stabbing pains would come next. Her hands trembled as she dug through her uniform pockets for her nitroglycerin tablets. "One of John's patients has a rare form of pneumonia."

"Is that right?" Bogle pushed away from the door frame and entered the room. Anne's eyes watered at the cloying scent of Lorraine's perfume. "I could wipe that smile off of your face."

Anne nodded, shivering.

Reaching into her blazer, Bogle removed a folded paper from her pocket. She looked at it briefly and then slammed it on the side table. "Apparently, patient care doesn't" interest John that much. He left for a family emergency. Cover his assignment."

Anne grimaced in pain as she leaned against her chair. If she didn't take her pills soon, she was heading for trouble.

"No problem." She pushed the words out between clenched teeth. "I hope things turn out all right for him."

"He said his son had an adverse reaction to his medicine. I'll give him a reaction." Bogle strode toward the door, shaking her fist. "This family leave policy only stretches so far. Next time, I'm firing him."

Bogle left and Anne bolted to the ladies' room. The pain had a stranglehold on her chest, and her ability to breathe. Loosening her collar, she glanced around the room. The stalls stood open and vacant, but the mechanical eye over the sinks maintained constant surveillance.

Balling her fist around her bottle of nitroglycerin tablets, she slipped them under her tongue. Waiting for them to dissolve, she stared at her reflection in the mirror. Widened green eyes tinged with yellow looked back at her through folds of pallid skin. Wisps of brown hair circled her angular features. According to her mother, she inherited her eyes, face, and physique from her father, who was an Athyrian extraterrestrial.

Scalp transplants and fat grafts rounded out Anne's features, making her look almost human. Right now, she didn't give a damn about her complexion. She was far more concerned about the pain. How soon would the pills work?

She never disclosed her species or her health problems to management. She wouldn't give them an excuse to fire her. Unemployment soared to thirty percent and her medical history alone could jeopardize her career. Although she just turned 35, the past few years were a struggle with angina and an irregular heartbeat. The attacks were getting more frequent, reminding her she was heading for a showdown with her heart condition.

Once the pain eased up, she left the restroom and cut through the Forgotten Ward to get back to the intensive care unit. Patients lined the cold, tiled walls, crying out for help as she passed. They wanted pain medicine. Cratered sores weeping green pus peppered one man's body from head to toe. A woman thrashed in bed, despite her leather restraints, her sheets caked with dried blood. A foul odor permeated everything – sickly sweet and decayed sour. Administration arranged for patients whose money and insurance ran out to transfer here. They ordered the staff to forget about these patients and their care, thus earning this ward the unfortunate moniker of "Forgotten Ward."

Anne rubbed her arms, trembling. Her mother screamed that same way during the last weeks of her life. The doctors mustered an army of antibiotics to fight the necrotizing fasciitis – a virulent infection that eroded the flesh and nerve endings in her mother's body. Nothing helped, not even surgery. Her mother died a skeletal figure writhing in agony.

Despite the ward's 70 degree temperature, chills shivered through Anne's body. The 2050 laws ruled lack of funds could remove a person's right to medical care. Here at Bridgestone Hospital, the administration gave such patients a week's grace period. The patient continued to receive attention during that week, but in a room with a window facing the Forgotten Ward. Administration theorized that watching the indigent patients writhe in bed, listening to their screams through a wall intercom, and inhaling their foul odors through an air vent might motivate delinquent patients to find money for their care.

Shivers settled in Anne's shoulders and neck as she contemplated her treatment plan for the forgotten patients, secure in her robot's network. Bogle claimed tampering with any hospital equipment would set off alarms, but Anne taught herself how to navigate the labyrinth of networks and computers as a child. It was easy to disconnect and reconnect the wires needed to override the alarms. After resetting the dials, she installed software she built to give the impoverished patients medicine. Her program gave them a measure of comfort and, occasionally, recovery.

Helping these patients eased her guilt over her failure to save her mother. Her piercing screams would haunt Anne's dreams forever.

Anne's unique talents endeared her to her co-workers — Paul, John, and Chloe — who invited her to lunch breaks and sometimes to their homes. On Bogle's days off, they covered her slot so she could look after the forgotten patients herself. She thanked them with gifts of homemade disks and software, despite it being unnecessary. Her coworkers' widened eyes betrayed a potent fear they could wind up sick and penniless one day.

All conversation stopped when Bogle came through their floor. Patient care kept everyone busy, even if they weren't working with patients. According to Chloe, patient care meant staying out of Bogle's way.

Bogle earned the nickname "Specter of Death" among the long-term care patients. She initiated most transfers to the Forgotten Ward and kept a list of all treatment orders. In the Forgotten Ward, all treatments went on hold, whether life support or custodial care.

After morning rounds, Anne went to the nurses' station to chart. Chloe's bright blue e-book reader was open on the desk. On its screen, the title, *35,000 Athyrians Disguised as Humans* leaped out at her. Anne read everything she could find about the Athyrians, hoping to understand that part of herself.

According to this article, a comet destroyed the Athyrian home planet of Athyr. Migrating to Earth, they offered to share their cloning technology in return for permission to breed with humans. In the United States, the Athyrians infiltrated the highest level of government, medicine, and industry. The President called them "gentle beings," but other politicians accused them of creating another alien species with which to invade and control Earth. Those same politicians enacted the 2050 laws regarding patient care.

"Hypocrites," Anne whispered.

"Anne!" Bogle's sharp voice jolted her attention back to her surroundings. Bogle rapped on the desk where the other nurses were charting. Her face reddened, complimenting her close-cropped brown hair and jutting chin.

She looks like Adolf Hitler. She even talks like him.
"What's wrong, Ms. Hitler ... I mean, Bogle?"

Titters erupted from the other three nurses.

"Professionals don't spend time reading, nor do I find your sarcasm amusing." Fury edged Bogle's voice. "Consider this a verbal warning."

Anne's smile disintegrated like fingerprints wiped with disinfectant. Perspiration trickled down her forehead. She knuckled them aside. "The article mentioned cloning techniques. I thought it might be helpful."

"Why? We never work with those patients."

"We may have to one day." Anne wiped her head again. Why was she sweating so much? The pressure in her chest reared like an elephant standing on her sternum. She grabbed the back of a chair for support.

The other nurses looked up from their terminals.

"Anne, are you okay?" Chloe's blue eyes went wide with fright.

"Do me a favor, Chloe. Shut up!" Bogle's expression darkened like a storm cloud.

Anne's pain intensified with each intake of breath. The sweat dripped on her uniform. Nothing seemed real to her now, not even Bogle.

"Oh, no," she whispered to herself.

"What did you say?" Bogle shouted in her ear, and Anne gagged on her cloying odor. "I can charge you with insubordination, which merits a suspension."

"What suspension?" Anne clutched her chest, tears running down her face. She staggered toward the desk. "I've got to sit."

"Here, let me help you." Chloe rose from her seat.

Anne crumpled into Chloe's arms.

"Call Doctor Greene!" Chloe cried out as she eased Anne to the floor.

Anne choked out her thanks, even as hazy darkness closed in on her. Someone wheeled the code cart her way, just before the world went dark.

****

Shushing noises gentled Anne into consciousness. Blue corrugated hoses covered her face, making hissing sounds. They were attached to a ventilator breathing air into her through a tube. A monitor beeped to the thud of her heartbeat. Something must have gone wrong for her to need a ventilator. A scream lodged in her throat, setting off the ventilator's alarms.

The red plastic draping the glass door told Anne she was in the Cardiac Surgical Unit, even as the door slid open, admitting a man clothed in white. She couldn't tell who he was beneath his pressurized suit. His helmet revealed thin lips, mustache, and thick glasses, but no other features. Staff wore clothing like this around quarantined patients.

"Relax, Anne." He spoke with a clipped accent. "You had a bad dream."

More like a nightmare. Doesn't anyone believe in identifying themselves?

"I'm Doctor Greene," he introduced himself as if he read her thoughts. He laid a plastic sheet on the table to her left. "I run the cardiac and cloning programs here. We almost lost you. Your coronary artery and two other arteries had huge occlusions. Your DNA profile made you an excellent candidate for cloning, so we were able to clone and replace the blocked arteries. As we did so, a clot broke loose and caused the stroke now affecting your right side. That's the bad news."

He paused, letting out a deep sigh. "The next step will be to clone and transplant your damaged brain cells. This is a lengthier process, but afterwards, your impairments will resolve. By the time we're ready to transplant, I expect that your chest will have healed."

His explanation had raised oh, so many questions, but the breathing tube made talking impossible. Shifting her gaze, Anne made out numbers and letters on the sheet. Pointing with her left forefinger, she managed one question: *How long will all this take?*

"Three to six months," Greene replied. "The infarction and surgery took a huge toll on you."

Three to six months? Anne pointed again, then coughed, setting off another chorus of alarms. *I'll be lucky if my insurance will cover half the bill.*

"I expect a positive outcome from the cloning procedure." The sadness faded from Doctor Greene's voice. "You may feel better than you did before surgery."

Oh, yeah? Bogle has zero tolerance for anyone who uses sick time or any other kind of time. Tears filmed Anne's vision and rolled down her cheeks.

"We'll start weaning you from the ventilator." Doctor Greene edged toward the door, his way of ending the conversation. "Take each day as it comes."

Easy for you to say. After the doctor left, she nodded off to sleep, weeping noiselessly.

A voice shouted at her, stirring her to consciousness, and Anne gagged as someone yanked the tube from her throat. Her eyes snapped open and she burst into a coughing fit.

"Easy." A familiar voice filled her ears as soft hands slipped an oxygen mask on her face. It was Chloe, still dressed in the white pants and floral top of her regular uniform.

As her coughing subsided, Anne took in her surroundings. A computer screen sat on the table at the foot of her bed. Bouquets of shiny balloons bobbed against the wall, flashing the message, "We love you." Despite the gifts, something felt wrong. The hall outside her room was too quiet. Using her left arm, she pulled herself to a sitting position. Her right arm dangled uselessly by her side.

"What's going on?" Her voice came out thick and slurred.

"Nothing." Chloe smiled, but her dark gaze flitted from side to side. Her tanned face glistened with perspiration. "You're doing fine."

"Where's your isolation suit?" Uneasiness clenched in Anne's stomach. "Won't you get into trouble?"

Chloe laughed. "Most of the doctors know you don't have anything contagious. Doctor Greene's into overkill."

"You think so?" Anne's eyes widened. "Doctor Greene said I had a heart attack, bypass surgery, and a stroke. He spoke as if he had his nose in a text file. So if he found other nasty surprises, please tell me. I'd rather hear it from you."

"Okay, I'll level with you." Chloe glanced up and down the hall, closed the door, and turned off the wall intercom. "When the technicians typed and crossed your blood for transfusion, they found out about the Athyr DNA in your cells. They went public with their information."

"Oh, no!" Chills inched up Anne's spine, despite the blankets covering her. "Bogle's going to have a fit."

"She already has." Chloe leaned toward the bed. "Whatever she does, you didn't hear this from me."

"Hear what? Have I spooked everyone?"

"No, but Bogle sure has. Everyone's staying out of her way." Chloe's eyes darted toward the door. She let out a sigh. "Bogle announced she's streamlining the department. She reprimanded me for coming in late yesterday."

"That doesn't surprise me." Anne shifted positions, hoping to ease her sore chest incision. "She threatened to fire John before I had my heart attack."

"Yeah...Well, she's had it in for everyone since then. Doctor Greene overheard her yelling at you. He said her approach made administration and the hospital look bad, so he gave her a written warning." Chloe's eyes widened as she scanned the monitors. "I'm afraid I've upset you. Let's talk about something pleasant."

"I'd rather you tell me the truth, even if it's bad." Anne shuddered at the heart monitor's erratic beep. "How long have I been here?"

"Six weeks. Weaning you from the respirator took some work. But enough of the morbid stuff." Perching on Anne's bed, Chloe typed something on the keyboard. The screen went blank. Humming noises followed, and then images of white-coated Athyrians filled the room. "I know you've wanted to know more about your Athyrian heritage. You should find this interesting."

"Thank you. Also for the balloons. I appreciate everyone looking out for me."

"You've got more humanity than Bogle ever will." A tear slid down Chloe's cheek. "I wish I could make your problems go away."

"You can't. No one can. But I need a favor. Do you have a paper and pen?"

Chloe nodded. She handed Anne scrap paper and a pen.

"I don't expect my insurance to pay for all of my care. So I need you to go to my locker and get my purse." Using her left hand, she carefully printed some numbers and handed the paper to Chloe. "This is the code to my locker. Get my purse and have it ready in case Bogle asks for my cash card. I might need certain documents from my condo. Also..." She cast a baleful gaze at her hospital gown. "If you get a chance, could you pick up my pink bathrobe—it's in the closet—and check my mail?"

"Of course, I will." More tears slid down Chloe's face, and her breath hitched with noiseless sobs. "Hope you enjoy the video."

She tucked the scrap paper in her pocket and skittered from the room.

Anne sighed, glancing at the surveillance cameras. The last thing Chloe needed was to be caught crying. Bogle had zero tolerance for emotional displays.

Turning her attention to the video, she clicked on a button. Images of a laboratory rose up around her, and Anne watched a virtual Athyrian dressed in white fill test tubes with an unknown solution and store them in an incubator. His bulbous canary yellow eyes studied each specimen with the intensity of a well-trained scientist. With his smooth albino skin and pointed ears, he looked like he could be her father.

The images faded, and another took its place. In the next scene, an Athyrian lay on a table, surrounded by figures in hooded masks and gowns. They were transplanting skin and hair from a cadaver to make the Athyrian look human. While Anne watched, memories of her childhood surfaced, a time when she too had undergone similar procedures. In the sterile cubicle, nested in her mother arms, she put aside the knowledge of her present illness.

The smell of antiseptic toyed with her nostrils, waking the forgotten child within her, buried under multiple surgeries. Before the surgeries, her appearance made her a target for bullies. Her classmates got high off of meanness and weren't content with name-calling. They picked fistfights, too, and sometimes they used knives. Anne developed a strategy for handling the hitters, and her strategy could be deadly. Like the time she threw a lead disk at an attacker, cracking his nose.

Her mother explained that other children couldn't understand her because she was "special." She told Anne they would have to stick close together because of the divorce. She gentled Anne through the surgeries and school fights by taking her for long walks. During those times, Anne could talk about anything, and her mother listened without judgment. Oh, they had their moments—like the time one of Anne's homemade electronic toys smashed someone's window or arguments over clothes and curfew—but mostly her home was her refuge.

She missed her mother. She missed her laugh and the love in her mother's eyes when she bought Anne a microscope and other birthday gifts. Most of all, she missed the admiration in her voice when she signed Anne up for the Alpha class reserved for students with IQ's greater than 150. Her mother's devotion awakened Anne's interest in medicine.

Looking at her younger self through adult eyes, Anne could understand the harrowing ramifications of her heart condition. It meant needing special drugs and surgery that advertised her hybrid status. Calls must have gone out to an Athyrian clinic for blood transfusions – another advertisement. Worst of all, no matter what Chloe said, no matter how many surgeries she got, she would never become human. Tears filmed Anne's vision. Her left fist clenched, fingernails digging into her palms.

In the next program, a virtual doctor implanted fertilized hybrid eggs into a woman while she was asleep. Anne's mother said she went through the same procedure because she couldn't get pregnant, and her husband refused to admit he was shooting blanks. Their marriage soured during the pregnancy. He left when Anne was four, but she had dim recollections of his bellowing voice. Why did the Athyrians impregnate humans, anyway? Maybe they considered humans something to...

The sliding cubicle doors impinged on Anne's speculations. With shaky fingers, she hit the keyboard's *quit* button. The images faded as Bogle marched in, flanked by two security officers, all of them dressed as if they were headed for outer space, with their white pressurized suits.

"How are you, Anne?" Bogle's voice reeked with false concern.

Liquid fear ran through Anne's veins. "Better, I think. Doctor Greene believes cloning will enable me to make a full recovery."

"His plans will have to wait. We've got financial matters to discuss."

Anne gulped, her throat bone dry. "My insurance covers inpatient care for up to three months."

"Only if you have a job," Bogle said gravely. "I fired you the day you collapsed on your floor. When we hired you, you never informed anyone of your heart condition or your hybrid DNA."

"Let me ask you this. Would you have hired me if you knew?"

"No." Bogle shook her head. "I should send you to jail."

Anne gazed forlornly at her hands. So pale and tiny compared to Bogle's—small compared to most human adults. "You can't do that."

"Oh, can't I?" Bogle's voice sharpened. "The state's offering thousands of dollars for hybrids. I get bonuses every time I save the hospital money. Your insurance covered your emergency treatment and your surgery, but not the six weeks you've been here."

Six weeks? Have I been out of it that long? Anne rubbed her chin, thinking. "I've got thirty thousand in the bank. Chloe has my purse. She can give you my cash card."

"We don't need your cash card to get to your account," Bogle said with a dismissive wave of her hand. "Your funds have paid for your care thus far, but your bank account has gone dry. With a cloning procedure, you will need much more. Do you have other sources of money?"

Using the automatic control, Anne raised the head of her bed so she faced Bogle. Pain sizzled through her chest incision. It was six weeks old, partially healed, but she had a way to go. "My condo. I can ask my bank for a loan."

"I've called the banks and mortgage companies. No one will lend to an unemployed person. Do you have any life insurance, bonds, or stocks?"

Anne shook her head, breath hitching with sobs, only dimly aware of the erratic beeping on her heart monitor. "My condo should sell for two hundred thousand dollars."

"Two hundred thousand?" Bogle shook her head again. "I doubt it. With unemployment skyrocketing, one can hardly afford a shack." She unplugged Anne's heart monitor and IV pumps. "These men will transport you to the holding area. You've got a week to raise the cash. If you're lucky, you'll succeed. If you're luckier, you'll die because the experiments the government doctors do on hybrids can cause further brain damage. You could end up like a houseplant."

Moments later, the officers moved Anne into a closet-sized room. Her balloons and video disk went to Security's office. Bogle's orders, the officers explained. No gifts, no visitors, no comforts from home unless she came up with cash.

Just doing my job, ma'am.

The room came with a picture window and a close-up view of the Forgotten Ward.

One man had multiple myeloma. The new anti-cancer drugs Anne got for him, via her homemade program, were starting to help. With Anne's intervention out of the equation and his lack of funds, he was facing a slow, painful death. Another patient had infected pressure sores. No one dared offer him dressing changes, antibiotics or painkillers. The patients' cries smoked with mad fear and pain, haunting Anne's dreams. She would give anything for her cell phone or her watch so she could tell time. Bogle didn't allow these either. Every so often, she received a flavored strawberry drink, the same mixture for each meal. Without a clock, she couldn't tell the difference between breakfast time and supper time, or even between day and night.

Her mother earned a fortune as a scientist. Most of her savings went to pay doctor bills, but she left Anne her condo. It would kill Anne to sell it, but better to sell it than die in the Forgotten Ward. She called a realtor on her bedside phone, hoping someone would bid on the property. No one did. She snatched glances at the phone, hoping for a call, but the phone remained quiet as death.

After what could have been hours or days, a gloved hand shook Anne's shoulder. "Anne, wake up." The voice of her coworker, John, whispered near her. "We're busting you out of here."

Anne's eyes fluttered open. John wore a white pressurized suit. Turning, he moved a stretcher toward her bed.

"To where?"

"Chloe's house. We'll have to move fast."

"Wait. Cameras are watching. You'll get arrested."

"Paul's handling surveillance." John glanced toward the door. "He should be here any minute."

"Get a humanoid to move me. Less chance of getting caught."

"The robot programs can't access the holding area." The tension in John's voice discouraged further argument. With the help of a mechanical arm, he transferred Anne onto the stretcher. Outside, footsteps thudded down the hall. "That must be Paul now."

Another hooded figure burst in past the glass doors. "Come on, John, move it. We've only got fifteen minutes."

Seconds later, they wheeled her stretcher outside into a parking lot. Anne savored the fresh night air brushing her cheeks. A full moon overhead danced golden shadows over the parked vehicles. It was beautiful, after being cooped up for weeks in the hospital.

John and Paul walked her stretcher up a ramp into an ambulance van. After plopping behind the wheel, Paul keyed the engine, cut the flashing lights, and nudged the vehicle toward Sycamore Street, a four-lane thoroughfare. He jammed the engine into a roar and sped onto the street in a cloud of blue smoke.

Anne never expected to recuperate at Chloe's apartment. That would make it too easy for the police to catch up with her. She assumed the men would swap vehicles and drivers at Chloe's. Someone else might whisk her to an out-of-state friend, perhaps a kind person who owed Chloe a lot of favors. She never asked questions, and no one volunteered information because the van carried a surveillance device. She never got to consider further possibilities. Halfway toward Chloe's apartment, the shrill whistling of a police siren filled the air.

Gunfire exploded, and the ambulance swerved as air escaped the tires. Paul skidded to the shoulder, cursing. A blue car pulled up alongside the van. Its flashing lights cut red shadows onto the street. Hurried footsteps followed, and then a man wearing navy blue shone a flashlight through Paul's window.

"I received a report that your van's carrying a stolen specimen. "The officer then recited the van's license plate number.

Specimen? Terror speared through Anne. *Is that what I've become to society?*

"What specimen?" Paul shrugged. "I'm moving a patient. Doctor's orders."

Sitting by Anne's stretcher, John squeezed her hand and held his finger to his lips. Reaching into his back pocket, Paul handed the officer two plastic cards. "Here's her identification and her discharge orders for her care at home."

The officer reviewed the cards and frowned. "Someone made a terrible mistake. "Wait here. I'll get my men to send you another vehicle."

The officer talked on his phone, but the sound of squealing tires and clicking footsteps drowned out his voice. Feet wearing spiked heels, like the kind Bogle wore. Anne would recognize Bogle's gait anywhere.

"There's my van!" Bogle cried in a shrill voice.

"Lady, I don't know who you think you are." The officer heaved a ponderous sigh. "This fellow's transporting a patient."

"Is that what the driver told you?" Bogle's voice filled with contempt. She whipped out her license and other identification. "I am Lorraine Bogle, head administrator of nursing at Bridgestone Hospital. My staff used this van to transport someone against my orders. The 'patient' is a hybrid specimen."

The officer poked his flashlight into the van again. Anne squinted at the blinding light. "She looks human to me."

"She's had several operations to make her look human," Bogle told him. "If you want, I'll show you her file."

"Lorraine Bogle, you've done enough!" A booming male voice cut through the air. Older, with a clipped accent. He flashed a shiny card and removed the helmet, revealing his Athyrian features. "Doctor Zehl Greene. I'll take over from here."

Slowly and rather deliberately, the officer turned toward Paul. "Your patient involves government security. You and your assistant are under arrest."

"Anne has a life-threatening arrhythmia," Paul argued. "She needs her medicine."

"Don't worry, Paul, Anne will get her medicine," the Athyrian doctor assured him. He turned toward the officer. "I see no reason to press charges, but I want Ms. Bogle, John, and Paul escorted back to Bridgestone Hospital. I'll handle the patient."

Silence fell while the officers unlocked the van's doors. They wheeled Anne back onto the street. She looked at John and Paul with wide eyes. Why did they think they could help her get away without being caught? "Your plan almost worked."

"Almost doesn't cut it." John's voice cracked with shame. "For what it's worth, Anne, I'm sorry."

Anne lay motionless while a humanoid rolled her into another van. Doctor Greene and the officer conferred in hushed voices. Moments later, Doctor Greene and his driver continued down Sycamore Street, past the turnoff John would have made to go to Chloe's.

The slanted forward windows gave Anne a view of the thinning houses spaced apart by groves of trees. The van turned left down an S-shaped road. To her left stretched a labyrinth of trees. On her right, the street looked down into a lake surrounded by trees and grass. The water glittered like a sheet of ice.

Open fields stretched for miles after the lake, and then a white brick four-story building loomed ahead. The driver pulled into a driveway and parked so that the rear doors faced the entrance. The doors slid open, revealing a dimly lit tiled hall.

The humanoid wheeled Anne into a tiled room crowded with computers and other machinery. The lettering on the exits and entrances in the hall and room looked like Greek. The humanoid pushed her stretcher near a panel laden with dials and view screens, giving Anne a look at the printout on the view screen. More foreign lettering. This building must belong to the Athyrians.

Without explaining its contents, the humanoid set up a new IV drip. Anne gazed at the exit, wishing she could run, but her right side flopped like a rag doll.

Doctor Greene entered moments later, wearing an ordinary lab coat, shirt, and trousers. Understanding dawned. At Bridgestone, he wore the pressurized suit and glasses to disguise his Athyrian features.

"Good evening, Anne." He smiled warmly.

Tears came to Anne's eyes. She knuckled them aside. "Hello, Doctor Greene. That is what I should call you, or do you prefer 'Zehl'?"

"Zehl will do. I don't stand on any formality. I brought you here so we can begin the cloning process to repair the brain damage."

"I appreciate your intentions." Anne shifted her gaze toward the door. "Unfortunately, I lost my job, so I can't pay you."

"Let's consider this research." The doctor walked around her stretcher, studying her monitors. "You've got guts and brains, a vital combination when you employ Bridgestone's robots to serve your agenda." He laughed. "Lorraine Bogle is so stupid. You scheduled surgery on the indigent right under her nose, and she never caught onto you."

Anne giggled, but the laughter died in her throat when she considered the possibilities. Was he trying to put her at ease or was he fishing for information? Beyond the intensity in his eyes, he gave no clue to his emotions. After having a brief mental conference with herself, she decided that anyone who disliked Bogle couldn't be all bad, which sent her into a laughing fit. Bogle's stupidity and the way Anne managed to fool her was objectively hilarious.

"My three coworkers caught onto me," she admitted after her laughter subsided. "They covered for me and nicknamed me 'Brain.' Chloe even figured out that I was part Athyrian. Composing software programs from scratch came naturally to me."

Her smile faded. "With all the brains I am rumored to have, I couldn't find a way to save my mother, or even make her comfortable."

"Your mother had a virulent strain of fasciitis," Doctor Greene said gently. "This disease challenges scientists like me. So if you ever develop an effective treatment, please let me know.

"You spent hours in the hospital, sitting by your mother's bedside. You took a leave of absence from your work so you could care for her at home. She couldn't have asked for a better daughter."

Anne gasped. "You certainly did your homework."

"I would consider it disrespectful not to, especially since I'm about to reveal sensitive information.

Your birth was part of an experiment that went sour."
He paused as if to let this information sink in, and
then added, "I'm your biological father."

Anne started, gasping, and pulled the sheet up to
her neck. *I must be hearing things. All the stress from the
stroke, the surgery, and Bogle's behavior have made my
mind ripe for hallucinations.* "No, that's not possible."

"Your intelligence quota runs over two hundred,
typical for an Athyrian," Doctor Greene told her.
"You have our complexion, eyes, and DNA, but the
human grafts conceal your Athyrian features. It was
an amateur job. The average human wouldn't notice
the difference, but you still have our DNA. How can
you say it's not possible?"

"A human raised me." Trusting Doctor Greene as
an ally was one thing, but accepting him as her father
belonged in another universe. The idea had repercus-
sions she wasn't ready to face. "So you bred me in a
test tube, mixing your chromosomes with my mother's. That doesn't make you my father."

"No one bred you in a test tube. Your mother
wanted a child, and she couldn't conceive, so she
came to me. We conceived you in a way people have
done since the beginning of time, inside a hotel
room." Doctor Greene smiled. "You inherited your
mother's capability for love and your intellect from
me. It is a shame she didn't send you to medical school.
You would make an excellent doctor."

"Sometimes I wish I could have gone to medical
school. Maybe then I might have figured out a way
to..." Anne snapped her mouth shut with a shudder.

Confiding her dreams and hopes sounded like a prelude to familial bonding. "It sounds like you took advantage of my mother's vulnerability. Why? She never hurt anyone." Her voice hitched. "People hassled me at school and her marriage broke up because... because..."

"I know all about it." Doctor Greene leaned against the tiled wall and looked at Anne. "Your mother's marriage had gone sour when she came to me. She knew what I was when she consented. If she were alive now, what do you think she'd say?"

Anne sighed. "I don't think she'd complain. From what she told me, my father couldn't admit he was sterile."

"That's what I thought." Doctor Greene smiled like a teacher who had coaxed a difficult answer from a shy pupil. "We hoped to create a society that would blend in the best of Athyrians and humans. Maybe one day, the hybrids could positively influence government and technology. Why your mother? She was a healthy person without any genetic defects or bad habits." He sighed. "The project was a colossal failure, but what's done can't be undone. You've learned that in patient care, I'm sure."

"I'm afraid I have." Anne shuddered, trying hard to ignore the fact her Athyrian intellect earned her respect and enabled her to save lives.

Just not my mother's.

"I can't believe the government allowed you to make hybrids. How did you get away with it?"

"When the comet slammed into our planet, our soil became useless. Many of my people died. Earth offered a congenial environment." Doctor Greene sighed, his voice becoming dim and ancient. "My leader signed treaties with the President, allowing us to conduct our experiments. In return, we agreed to share our technology."

"Such as cloning."

"That's right. We tried to keep track of the hybrid babies. There were about five thousand. Half of them died after gestation, aborted during the first trimester. Another third disappeared after birth, bought or kidnapped by government agents." The doctor's voice saddened. "The remaining survivors developed heart conditions because their metabolism can't process complex fats and starches."

"Like me," Anne ventured in a small voice.

"Like you. Your friends took serious risks with your life when they tried to smuggle you from the hospital."

Anne shuddered as the icy fingers of terror inched up her spine. "Please leave my friends out of this. They were trying to keep me out of the Forgotten Ward."

"I am aware of that. I planned to move you out here once you were moved to the Forgotten Ward, but your friends jumped ahead of me. Chloe loves you like a sister, but she's always stuffing everyone with rich sweets. Those fatty foods can kill you, and no one understands that."

Doctor Greene heaved a sigh. "At least you've got friends. Most of the hybrids who've survived grew up lonely and bitter, wanting to be human, wanting to be Athyrian. Even you, Anne, have ambivalent feelings about your identity."

Anne glanced at her monitors, noted the symbols instead of numbers that told her vital signs, and looked back at Doctor Greene. "At work, you've had plenty of opportunities to identify yourself, but you didn't. Why not?"

"You weren't ready for the truth."

"I'm not sure I'm ready now." Anne lowered her gaze. Her limp arm and leg looked like relics of a career she once enjoyed. "Bogle couldn't wait to send me to the Forgotten Ward. Since when did money -- or lack of it — define someone's right to live?"

"Bridgestone Hospital lost a lot of money. My colleagues and I suggested rationing treatment to those who couldn't pay, meaning no elective procedures and longer waits for other treatment."

"Bogle didn't just ration treatment. She eliminated it. Every time I listen to the forgotten patients, I hear my mother screaming in agony. Worse, I couldn't do anything about it. The drugs only helped her a little bit." Anne swallowed hard, fighting back the tears. "No one asks to be poor."

"Anne, calm yourself." Doctor Greene nodded to the monitors. "Getting upset won't do you any good."

"I could have died in the Forgotten Ward," Anne persisted. "When someone's sick, you help them. You don't let them bleed to death."

"I had nothing to do with that law. My colleagues and I made a suggestion; your senators and Bogle ran with it." Doctor Greene's amber eyes met hers. "The horrors you went through illustrate humans' primitive temperament."

"Bogle makes humanity look bad."

"Someone hurt Lorraine Bogle a long time ago." His voice softened, conceding compassion. "It doesn't give her the right to attack people. Your principal about not letting people bleed — I assume this includes hybrids."

"Of course, it does."

"About a thousand hybrids are walled off in some laboratory or institution. I want to find them and treat their injuries." Doctor Greene glanced at Anne's monitors. "Whether you believe it or not, Athyrians feel compassion, but they express it differently. I will gladly proceed with your treatment, but I need your help in finding those hybrids."

Anne rubbed her chin with her good hand. "I can save you money by taking the treatment at Chloe's home," she offered.

"That won't do." Doctor Greene frowned. "Cloning should be done at a hospital."

"If you mean Bridgestone Hospital, I'll never feel safe with Bogle there. If you provide the text, I can teach myself and Chloe incubation and other procedures. She's a great nurse." She mustered a smile. "Come on, Doctor, you just said I have an Athyrian's IQ."

"It won't work. Chloe works full time, and cloning is too delicate a procedure for anyone to manage alone—even you. Lorraine Bogle has nothing to do with my clinic here. Chloe and your other friends are welcome to visit, call, and bring you things. Except..." He wagged his right forefinger. "Someone will be screening the edible gifts."

"Right, because refined starches and sugars..."Anne broke off, aware more important issues lay at stake. The memory of the indigent patients and their cries weighed heavy on her mind. Perhaps the 2050 laws could be overturned. What if her connections to Doctor Greene gave her a hammer with which to legalize treatment for the poor? "What I mean is, I will gladly take my treatment here and help you find the other hybrids."

Doctor Greene reached for his phone and punched in some numbers. While he dictated her medical history to the admissions clerk, Anne eased herself against her pillows, a satisfied smile tugging at her lips.

For the first time since she began working as a nurse, she felt something other than the sting of injustice and the despair of being unable to help those she first became a nurse to save. Now, instead of relentless fury and sorrow, she felt genuine hope.

With her newfound lease on life and Doctor Greene's assistance, perhaps the Forgotten Ward and its patients would no longer be forgotten. Maybe, for the first time, they could all be remembered.

That was a future she could make happen, and it made every moment of pain worth suffering.

About the Contributors

Barbara Custer:

Barbara lives near Philadelphia, Pennsylvania, where she's worked as a respiratory therapist. She enjoys fright flicks and working on horror and science fiction tales. She's published *Night to Dawn* magazine since 2004.

Other books by Barbara include *Twilight Healer, City of Brotherly Death, Infinite Sight, When Blood Reigns,* and *Steel Rose*; also novellas *Close Liaisons* and *Life Raft: Earth.* She enjoys bringing her medical background to the printed page, and then blending it with supernatural horror. She maintains a presence on Facebook, LinkedIn, Twitter, and The Writers Coffeehouse forum. Look for the photos with the Mylar balloons, and you'll find her.

You can email her at barbaracuster@hotmail.com. Visit her at:

www.bloodredshadow.com

www.facebook.com/barbara.custer

L. M. Labat:

Born in 1993, L. M. Labat stems from New Orleans, Louisiana. From the struggles of a broken family and surviving life-threatening events, Labat found refuge within the arts while delving into the fields of medicine, psychology, and the occult. While combining illustration and literature, L. M. was able to cope with endless nightmares as well as hone in on artistic techniques. From confronting the past to facing new shadows, this author gladly invites audiences into the horror of *The Sanguinarian Id*.